The Sea of Angles

C. J. Jones

Cider Press

North Wales

To June,
a very dear friend

The first thing to have in a library is a shelf. From time to time, this can be decorated with literature. But the shelf is the main thing.

F. P. Dunne

CONTENTS

CHAPTER 1

RITES OF PASSAGE

*

Dai Llewellyn-Jones had pulled summer behind him on his tractor earlier in the year and now he dragged the blustering autumn down the high road. The seasons obediently follow the tractor.

It was the year of the great flood in North Wales when Beaumaris was underwater and part of the North Wales coast mainline was swept away. Four cars passing the *gwasanaethau* sign at Bangor were lifted by the water and

11

floated merrily downhill to the Menai Strait. There was a drunk, turned out of the Garth pub that Friday night, who saw them sailing down the strait to the estuary at Penrhyn. But a garage twenty miles away, hoping to get one up on its competitors, said that all four cars turned up on its forecourt with sodden engines and wet brakes.

It was that same night that Tudur Llewellyn-Jones, son of Dai, was driving to the Empire Hotel in Llandudno. Two police officers in luminous yellow jackets and galoshes told him to turn back near the *gwasanaethau* sign, not to go as far as the roundabout, or his car would be following the four others swept down the road to the narrow strait of water which joins sea to sea.

Tudur drove backwards along the central reservation, keeping two of his wheels on the driver's side high and dry out of the water when both of his windscreen wipers broke, and he inched through thirty miles of gridlocked cars on the A55 in blinding wet to keep his dinner reservation.

Hearing the hotel's grand piano and seeing the bare bodied women framed in pictures on the walls, he proposed marriage to Eiluned Lloyd-Jones because they were both under siege and surrounded by water. It is characteristic of humans that in the face of peril they tend to form alliances. Nor is it coincidence, I believe, that the animals and humans went two by two into the ark in the original flood. In the face of this great flood the humans acted no differently and immediately paired up where they could.

The North Wales coastline has been shaped directly by the hands of God, with the close proximity, the double blessing, of sea and mountains together in the same place. It has a language spoken by no one else anywhere in the world, except a few stray sons in Patagonia.

If the language were not proof enough of its special status, once can name at least a dozen others: The abundance of holy places and shrines; the multiplicity of freshwater drinking wells; the incomparable taste of Welsh lamb (far superior to New Zealand baby mutton); the unparalleled flavour of Welsh black beef (so good that the Scots take the Welsh beef cattle for the last few weeks of their rearing and pass the beef off as their own); spectacular outcrops sticking up strangely in the landscape like burgeoning mountains; and the temperament of the natives which is always content to stay at home, convinced that nowhere on earth matches the perfection of Anglesey, Gwynedd, Clwyd, (grudgingly) Powys, and (just possibly) Denbighshire. And this view is indisputably true.

When Dai pulled winter with its snow and ice pellets onto the scene at twenty miles per hour with his tractor and his flashing light, holding up the faster vehicles on the A5025, no one was grateful. The harsh winds of winter make it an unwelcome season when it comes.

Dai's farmyard is surrounded by Christmas trees. Each year he plants the Christmas tree outside, now denuded of its shiny ornaments and baubles, expecting it to die in the new year frost. But it defeats expectation and there is a forest of Christmas trees unwilling to expectorate their green souls at the farmer's insistence.

The turkey is hanging, lifeless, upside down, by its legs from a rope, waiting for the annual plucking. Anni performs the task carefully, reluctant to delegate even to capable Llewellyn hands, because the turkey breast is delicate, easily damaged by careless plucking. She warms the turkey and her own hands before the plucking. A warm turkey always plucks better.

Uncle Jac, the Jesuit priest from Clwyd, comes to stay at Christmas. Each year it's the same. Because Uncle Jac brings the Lord with him when he comes, he does not expect to bring presents and every year he says thank you to Anni, Dai's wife, for Christmas dinner and sits smiling, unabashed, as presents are handed round, including one from Dai and Anni to him.

Tudur and his brother, young enough to be perturbed by this undemocratic state of affairs and not overly impressed by the Lord, discuss the matter mutinously from time to time. Tudur decides that as second man in the house but without the host's duty of politeness, he will take a hand in matters. When Uncle Jac says after the festive lunch, "Why thank you Anni for a sumptuous lunch as usual. You've done us proud," Tudur immediately pipes up, "And thank you Uncle Jac for the present."

If ever a man lived up to the term jesuitical, it is Uncle Jac who brazenly responds, "Why you're welcome Tudur."

Huw laughs behind his hand at his brazen uncle. "Nice try, Tudur," he whispers.

As the brandy is poured over the dome of Christmas pudding and set alight with a match, Gwyneth the baby says, "Can I have fire on my pudding?"

Anni, Dai's wife, her two hips wider than her shoulders, sits in the armchair, her thick blue veined legs raised on the footstool, falling asleep, dreaming of escaping cows and tinkling cow bells, forgetting the creamy fluffy white rice pudding baking in the oven with its brown crust of nutmeg.

Dai is a true son of the land. He has stayed where God first put him on this earth. He does not presume to know better than his creator and has never left this spot on Ynys Môn, his island home. Tudur is a renegade. He climbed Mount Snowdon. Dai has never climbed Mount Snowdon. Tudur phoned his father from the peak.

"I'm very high up now. I'm sure I can see you in the kitchen. I must be higher than I thought. An airline pilot just waved."

Huw is a better son. He drinks beer in the garden with his father, amidst the flies, enjoying the smell of honeysuckle around the farmyard gate. In the summer he goes through a rite of passage and becomes a man. He deliberately sets fire to the gorse with matches. Like the flaming end of a rocket at lift off, Holyhead mountain goes up in flames. Fuelled by

14

parched gorse and dry bracken, red and yellow Catherine wheels of flame leap into space. In the morning charred black hillock and smoke remain.

When he was a boy, Dai, along with Stef Evans, a respected member of the community, a teacher, and also a local councillor, set fire to the gorse. It is an institution like the sapping of apples.

"Oh I set it alight, the mountain. It's what all school boys do," says Dai. It's the way a boy passes from boyhood to manhood in the country.

On the other side of the bay, over near Porth Swtan, the acres of gorse go on fire when drunken revellers stumbling home from the pub along unlit farm tracks throw matches after lighting cigarettes. Fire, conflagrations, bigger than anything they expected to light. And blaring headlights catch frightened rabbits' eyes in the dark, as the racing fire engine's big black wheels set a hedgehog or two spinning on the road, make the pheasants roosting in the bushes rise squawking out of the branches, and leave a fox dead in the ditch.

"Boys have got to stop firing the mountain," the fire chief booms, his big hand slapping the table. They print his views in black type in the local newspaper. There is a radio debate. Stef Evans sticks up for the boys.

"It's an institution," he says. "All boys do it."

Fire in the gorse does a better job of clearing the encroaching prickly bush than any old tractor which gets stymied by a bit of sloping hillside or rocky outcrop. The charring doesn't last long and before you know it the hillside looks as though it has been washed green again.

Mist rises spookily from the air vents of the sea around the charred mountain which is beginning to live and grow green once more.

The ants' nest under Dai's flagstone patio begins to erupt with fliers. The green fern in his garden eases itself from rock to rock, its frondy hands clambering, gripping

15

here, seizing a handhold there, making itself comfortable in the crevices of rocks limed white with the excreta of seagulls and other birds.

There are four other Llewellyn-Jones's growing up into Tudur's hand-me-downs. And when spring arrives with the lambs, the season nudging behind Dai's tractor, impatient for arrival, Huw at fifteen is ready for graduation to manhood.

In Anni's laundry room there is a butterfly stuck to the hard floor with glue. Or it looks glued in place because its wings are poised like aeroplane wings for flight. But there is no wind to fan them any longer. And if a gentle breeze came the patterned wings, looking like the rolls of fabric carelessly unrolled by Welsh housewives on the market seller's stall at Llangefni, would topple with a whisper. Dead. But nobody touches the butterfly. It stays where it is.

It is the same week the Catholic priest of their parish crawls across his lawn in his fantastic Homer Simpson blue underpants to seduce a young virgin, until his mother screams piercingly, "Sh . . sh . . shocking," from the patio doors. But this is his dream and not real and only comes in useful later on.

Alun, Rhodri, and Gwyneth Llewellyn-Jones run out of games. During winter they played leaving a bunch of mistletoe out on the road, with a long piece of twine attached, which they twitched to bring the mistletoe back whenever a passer-by stooped to take it home for kissing under. If anyone on the road complains about the unfairness of this game Rhodri shouts, "Get Dad."

Now they play who can find the most interesting thing in the farmyard. When the time for collecting things is up and they all get together on the garage roof to see who has the most interesting things in their collection, they realise they haven't voted for a judge. They've all been collecting things and each of them thinks that they have the most interesting thing, but there isn't anyone left over to decide between them.

They put the question of a judge on one side to look at the interesting things.

Rhodri has a square object, shaped like a times table square. It is a broken piece of a grid which has been stopping chunks of food and other debris from falling down the drain. Alun has red and green coloured smooth pieces of something which he thinks are jewels, rubies or emeralds. No one puts him right or says you don't get rubies and emeralds lying about on the driveway of ordinary folk.

The baby, Gwyneth, has gone for nature in her interesting things, a pine cone fallen off a tree, one of those orange flowers which opens in the sunshine and closes up when it starts to rain, and a dead bee.

Anni is woken from her dreams of fleeing cows with their neck bells ringing by the sound of a helicopter. Landing in one of the fields the rotor blades are whirring, causing a massive draught that bends the trees. Anni runs out to complain about the noise. They must leave. Landing on private property.

"You can't land here. Don't you know there is an airfield over at Valley?"

The pilot tells her that a neighbour has phoned for assistance. There is a man fallen down in the field. Anni pooh poohs the notion. Why has her nap been interrupted?

The helicopter has been called out by the hospital at Bangor, Ysbyty Gwynedd.

"An ambulance is on its way," says the pilot, "but the helicopter is quicker."

Quicker at arriving and airlifting a sick man to the hospital nearly thirty miles away. Finally Anni takes a look over the hedge into the field. Dai is the man who has dropped down into the ploughed furrow.

17

There is only room in the helicopter for Dai. If any of the family wish to go to hospital they will have to drive by car.

I once watched a tragi-comic scene played out on the television news years ago with the death of the Ayatollah Khomeini. The helicopter bearing the dead Ayatollah was surrounded by mourners and weepers who grasped at the helicopter as it tried to take off, pulling on its stabilisers until the craft tipped, delivering the wrapped body out of the helicopter and into the arms of the waiting crowd. And then there was a scrum, and a pulling and a pushing of the body which went one way and then another, in and out of the helicopter, astonishing television viewers around the world.

Despite their grief at their father's illness, the Llewellyn-Jones's remain dignified. They do not grab at the helicopter, tip it up, or insist on overloading the craft with extra persons. Tudur brings the car around, to take his mother to the hospital.

As one life falters another starts. A child is conceived by Tudur and Eiluned who got married in the spring. That conception takes place is a miracle because the Llewellyn-Jones's are Catholics. Dai and his sons drink alcoholic liquor. The Lloyd-Jones's are Chapel and do not drink. But Eiluned cannot risk waiting another season for a proposal of marriage from a more suitable Chapel young man. Young Welshmen of her own age with prospects, work, are rare in this part of the world. Tudur, the eldest son, will inherit the ploughed furrows, the tractors that drag the seasons through the quartered year, and the farmyard surrounded by Christmas trees.

Like all good Celtic nations, Wales has a long history of spirit distillation, starting back in the fourth century with Reaullt Hir of Bardsey Island. The spirit, quite rightly, was known in those days as *aqua-vitae* (or *gwirod* in Welsh). Unfortunately spirit production halted in the nineteenth century due to the influence of Chapel and "Temperance," but the old spirit is, thankfully, making a strong comeback as religious mania recedes and the ancient Celtic temperament raises its head again along with the language.

The Catholic priest is invited to marry them. Tudur, as a Catholic, has to have a Catholic ceremony. And Eiluned lets the bread of the holy Eucharist dissolve in her mouth as her husband's ancestors have done since long before the dissolution of the monasteries.

The priest, Father Tristan, marries them with his fantastic blue zinging underpants underneath his vestments. His dreams are potent prophecies.

Eiluned knows that this is a land shaped personally by the hand of God. The archangels may have had a hand in forming other nations, but this one was shaped by God alone. For this reason she is willing to return to the old religion that existed before Chapel.

The oldest rocks in the world underpin this coast. Old. Old. Old. Everything is old. Even the turning of the seasons brought in by farmers. Before tractors, autumn came on the point of a pitchfork and landed on a stack of hay, winter saw itself off with a shiver, spring was ushered in with the calves, and in summer boys relinquished their boyhood when the mountain flared up in a pyre of dancing orange flames, and emerged as men when the mountain began to spring gorse again on its charred ashy slopes.

CHAPTER 2

DEAD DOGS AND MEAT PIES

*

Dai is a man of few words. He uses them sparingly, afraid that if he utters too many he will use them all up. His father before him was also a man of few words and Dai's mother died during his childhood, so that if it were not for an extraordinary stroke of good fortune it might not have been possible for Dai to have married since he was not a man of enough words to have put the proposal to anyone.

It was Anni who had to take charge of the relationship. Like Hera of the Olympian gods, Anni married her near relation. Not quite her brother, but a first cousin who spoke no English and only a few words of Welsh. The acquaintance began with pies. Big solid meat pies; Welsh lamb, potato and gravy surrounded by a golden crust of pastry. Lots of them.

Anni's mother made the pies and sent the little girl in knee high socks to the farm next door with its lonely male occupants, a father and two sons. Anni's mother, Blodwen,

20

was a good woman with a heart of pity for three men on their own who couldn't cook. Neither man nor boys being able to cook, they were lean years until Anni started visiting and supplying them with pies.

There was magic in those pies. Either there were magic herbs growing in Blodwen's kitchen garden which flavoured the Welsh lamb pies with a taste so succulent, so otherworldly, that no pies anywhere else on Ynys Môn could compete with the pies that Anni brought to their kitchen or, more likely, Anni crossed the gypsy's hand with silver for a lucky charm. Since there can only be one true explanation, if it is not the first it is the second, and if it is not the second it is the first.

I incline to the second explanation myself as, from the beginning, Anni said to herself inwardly that she liked a man of few words and since she is a woman of many words herself it is better that her husband utters not too many, or their words would shove up against each other and compete for space.

Anni is well-known for her love of dogs. She has grown up with dogs all her life. Dai still uses dogs to round up his sheep, unlike Tudur who speeds around his father's acres on a three-wheeled motorbike, taking the field corners with the expertise of any Formula 1 driver. There is no one like Tudur for taking a corner on two wheels and maintaining his balance. The sheep, as in the Bible passage, know their master's voice, and they respond to Tudur's, "Yip, yip, yip," and roaring engine with more respect than they show to Dai and his dogs.

Anni's foible is a love of dogs totally unsuited to farm life. Dai is ashamed of his wife's love of toy dogs. His wife's Chihuahua, barely six inches off the ground, proved invisible to a man standing six feet and more off the ground. After treading on the six inch high canine creature time and again, Dai began to throw it fatty snacks, red meat, eggs, and chocolate, under the table. Sneakily, without Anni's knowledge, Dai began to fatten up the tiny dog in an attempt to make it visible. It grew visible as its girth thickened but its fat sides caused the dog to wheeze and pant for air when waddling about the kitchen.

On the rare occasions that Snodgrass the Chihuahua managed to waddle into the farmyard for air, it was taunted by the local boys who hung over the farmyard wall shouting out, "It's a rat, it's a rat," at the poor unfortunate Snodgrass.

The Chihuahua met its end under the rear wheels of Dai's tractor when he reversed into the farmyard when, for all his conscientious programme of fattening, he was unable to perceive the small fat dog under his wheels.

The Chihuahua was succeeded by a slightly larger dog and one with correspondingly larger yaps; a white Shih Tzu. This too met its end under a farm vehicle's wheels and Dai, perceiving that his wife's tolerance for his accident with her dog might turn to unjustified suspicion with the advent of a second, quietly buried the dog in an outlying field and omitted to mention its death. Suspicion therefore fell on some unknown persons driving recklessly on the highway and who lacked courage to report a dog's death. It was concluded by Anni that Pom Pom had been knocked down by someone and lay buried somewhere in some grey ditch; a suspicion not far from the truth.

"Poor Pom Pom," she would sigh in the evenings, stabbing at the fire with the poker, as though she were merely dealing out what a dog-killer deserved. "I wonder what happened to her?"

And then, "You're sitting too near the fire, Dai," as the farmer's cheeks mottled with florets of colour.

Anni's brother, Wyn, on the neighbouring farm, is a man of many words like his sister, and of a liking for strong drink. When his temper flares the words rise into the air with projectile force, like hot water from a geyser. When it comes to pub turning out time, the Welsh denizens of the hill above the pub are treated to a ringside seat, with Wyn circling his drunken opponent with balled fists and eyes narrowed in the moonlight. The moon's influence on the affairs of man is well known and as soon as the moon waxes, Wyn can be found brawling on the floor of the pub car park.

There are no ropes at the pub, but a grey dry-stone wall, built by master dry-stone waller Dafydd Rhys. That stone wall is a monument to the skill of a man who has built thousands of walls in his building career. Its stones, held cemented together only with Dafydd's skill and no drop of mortar, have held up Wyn's body these past thirty years as he hangs over the parapet and empties the liquid contents of his belly out onto Steffan Bach's field.

For those who rejoice at the skill of modern engineering which enables a tractor to run at incredible speeds, the sight of Wyn racing down his farm track to the pub at night would bring joy to the heart. With his belly lightened of some of its contents, he races back uphill at closing hour and, although not so fast uphill, he is fast enough to make the ruts in the road roar like thunder as the tractor hits them.

No self-respecting animal, bird, beast or man would risk walking up Wyn's farm track around the times of pub opening and closing. Even the pheasants, stupidest of birds, shout warnings to each other at the time of the last orders bell.

.

CHAPTER 3

MY LEARNED FRIEND

*

There are doings that take place on the tops of mountains and hills that are not heard of anywhere else. This is no doubt due to the health-giving properties and purity of the air in these elevated places. The effect I believe is something similar to the ancient rite of trepanning. Letting air to the brain appears to bestow some superior mental qualities or wisdom denied to others.

It has often been said, quite wrongly, by off-islanders that Anglesey is flat. This is entirely false. It is true that there are points from which one can see across the whole isle to the sea and mountains on the other side, but these vistas actually take place from the vantage point of an elevation. Or hill.

And the good Doctor Hughes, responsible for the health of most of the inhabitants of this part of Anglesey, and who walks and cycles regularly for the sake of his own health, tells anyone who will listen that this fair isle is by no means flat. There are enough hills to raise his pulse rate sufficiently to alarm his heart when he takes his daily constitutional.

There is an architect and his wife occupying the best part of a nearby hill. And there is a barrister and her husband occupying the lower slope. The architect's family have a view over the top of the lawyer's house, but the advantage of height is nullified in this particular case because, in fact, the two families have exactly the same view out to sea at a point where there is nothing but a blue, or grey (the colour being entirely dependent on the weather) blanket of sea stretching out in all directions.

There is therefore great harmony between the two families who are not inclined to compete with their neighbours over the superiority of their view, since the same grey (or blue) blanket may be seen either to the left, or to the right, or in front, all the way to the horizon.

There are spectacular moons above Holyhead mountain shaped like shortbread petticoat tails of the sort that come in boxes off the top shelf of the Spar shop at Valley. The architect's roof is limed white from the excreta of seagulls that make noises like squeaky toys pressed hard in the middle as they fly over.

When Eirian, the lawyer, speeds across the bridge to Holy Island in her car she notices a trail of colourful bits of paper being ejected from the drain in the wall into a gully. Close inspection shows that the trail is in fact not waste paper but a line of canoes that come speeding on the current through the low down gap in the wall of the bridge. If there is any skill in manoeuvring through a small gap in a wall into the ditch, it is not immediately apparent to a novice because the twitching kayaks spin rather helplessly in the jet of water. But they descend from the foaming jet stream at a speed that makes Eirian the lawyer applaud their daring because each canoe lands neatly with the canoeist upright.

The urge to kayak is irresistible if you have ever seen it done on rapids and not on a children's pond or children's

25

lake. Fired with enthusiasm, Eirian buys a little red kayak for canoeing the waves at Porth Swtan. This is the bay near Holyhead where big waves come in after the ferry goes to Ireland. The little red canoe is for riding the surf that arrives in the wake of the big boat heading west.

The waves are bigger than Eirian expects. The wave that runs towards her with a hoover sucking motion causes the greatest fright as she envisages herself tumbling head over heels and heels over head, just as she did in Friday games lessons at Bodedern secondary school. The hoover sucking motion seems to work in reverse, as when the bag of the vacuum cleaner is full and begins spitting out dirt rather than picking it up. The suction moves her closer to the beach which, on this sultry August weekend, is packed as closely with children as a punnet is with mustard and cress.

When the punnet is washed in running water, all the little mustard balls fall out and drop into the sink, like heads dropping from the guillotine in the Reign of Terror. So it is on the beach when Eirian is swept by the tide onto a mass of bobbing heads on the edge of the shore.

With the ingrained caution of a lawyer she shouts a warning before capsizing helplessly onto the swimmers.

"Get out of the way. I don't want anyone to get hurt."

By some freak of wind or noisy pounding of the waves, as when a mobile phone loses its signal and cuts out one word in four, delivering a highly ambiguous sentence, a current of air distorts her words into, "Get out of the way you fat arses."

Fortunately, although bruised and indignant, no one is badly hurt. And once Eirian, with her lawyer's caution, has ascertained that she will not be liable for any death or serious injury, she picks up the little red canoe and flees along the cliff path.

As a lawyer she knows all too well about compensation claims. She has no dangerous sports insurance and does not want to appear before His Honour in court in the guise of the Defendant instead of as My Learned Friend.

Naturally, as the legal profession always attracts the cleverest brains, Eirian's estimation of her own merits is justifiably great. Her husband's family have not always paid the deference or respect due to her fine legal mind, as she very often reminds him when he comes home tired from work at night after supervising his employees picking cockles on the beach.

Their wedding day cake on that joyous occasion had come all the way from Harrods, travelling 250 miles in state from London to Holyhead. The cake was met by a reception committee, but after the greetings and polite applause were over and the lid of the box lifted to expose the magnificent wedding cake, there were shrieks of horror from Eirian. Her shouts in Welsh were loud but unintelligible to the courier of the beautiful cake and her fiancé had to translate, apologetically, to the cake bearer that the cake was unacceptable to his wife.

The cake, coming as it had in grand style, arriving like royalty from London, had attracted a crowd of curious onlookers who were not sure what the occasion might be but had joined in the supposed festivities anyway. Those who spoke Welsh were treated to a tirade of words from Eirian on the deficiency of the huge snowy creation being lifted out of the van. At any other time such a beautiful cake would have elicited gasps of admiration and handclaps from the spectators but, to the puzzlement of those latecomers just tagging themselves on at the back of the crowd, it seemed that the visitor from London had failed to be a crowd-pleaser.

Craning their necks to see over the heads of the spectators in the front rows, they were too far back to catch a few derisive comments issuing from Eirian's prospective brother-in-law that Eirian's brains had, "Busted out of her

27

head at last. She always had too many brains for her own good that girl."

Mr Jenkins, the bridegroom's father's comments were, however, audible to those in the back row who had arrived late for the entertainment.

"It's all the fault of that Oxford education," he blustered in Welsh. "What was wrong with the local university, that's what I'd like to know? Not good enough for us now she's been mixing in high circles. Those stuck up airs and graces. What's wrong with a Welsh cake? Coming all the way from London indeed."

One or two of the more spiteful citizens have suggested that Mr Jenkins's eyes are perpetually red rimmed due to his imbibing too much hard liquor. However it may well have been the chilly Welsh wind from which Mr Jenkins suffered, evidenced by his wrapping his limbs up well. So well in fact that he appeared to have no neck between his head and his shoulders.

The babble of two languages competing and the rising shrieks due to each individual's wish to ensure that he or she was heard, led to such a confusion that for a while no one was quite sure what the issues were or how they were to be resolved.

Finally it emerged that the source of the trouble was the colour of the ribbons on the wedding cake and the colour of the icing used to write the bride and groom's names on the top of the cake.

Eirian's mother was offering consolation to her daughter, in Welsh, and issuing instructions to the van driver in English.

"It's a beautiful cake," said Eirian's mother in Welsh.

"But it's not what I wanted," screamed Eirian.

It took a few minutes for the van driver to register the protest because Eirian's fiancé had to translate it from Welsh into English.

"They're bringing Mr Al-Fayed himself," said Eirian's mother. "They're bringing him to the phone. He's coming directly."

"Ribbons and icing," said Mr Jenkins bitterly.

"Mr Fayed is coming downstairs," Eirian's mother assured her. "He will take care of it personally. I've spoken to six assistants and they're bringing Mr Fayed."

"The best ingredients. Personally overseen by the head chef," but the van driver's words are seized by the wind and carried off into the air. No one hears them.

A seagull circles overhead, mewling and cackling, looking for pickings. It sees nothing worth eating and disgustedly drops a load from its undercarriage onto the van driver's window.

"Here," says the van driver. "Get off."
He wipes the windscreen with a beautiful green and gold cloth.

"I'm sending it back," screamed Eirian. "I want another one."

"I hope it will be alright," Eirian's intended muttered.

"What? Her brains or the cake?"

But whoever had uttered the last remark was not discovered, as the unwelcome visitor from London was clapped back into the vehicle, and the speaker's words were lost in the roar of the engine and the crash of the gears as the van sped off on its return journey.

CHAPTER 4

THE BOY WHO WAS A
PICTURE BOOK

List of contents:-

Morgan Davies has trouble attaching the summer season to his tractor.

He only goes to sleep with a thick padlock on his door.

Bryn Davies resembles a cooked sausage.

He had ankles like notepads, and cat and dog shaped holes in his clothes.

How it is better not to wear your sister's stocking on your head if you want to fit into society.

How jagged toe nails can snag your bedclothes.

The story of Bryn Davies's life is tattooed across his body.

Morwena Davies has magic dusters.

Morwena Davies's search for a husband.

The problems of having cold feet at night and the necessity of bed socks.

*

There is a part of Anglesey where summer always comes later than on the rest of the isle. This is the area around the Black Lion pub which is now defunct so far as the licensed premises is concerned, as a hermit crab shell is when its owner has discarded it for an alternative dwelling.

The reason that summer misses its curtain call is that Morgan Davies is always late attaching the season to his tractor and when he finally does agree to bring it, it comes slowly, reluctantly, in that part of the world, almost frightened into flight by the taciturn, grumpy farmer's ill-tempered looks as he jerks his tractor into gear and refuses to pull into the lay-bys along the road to let faster moving vehicles pass, despite a heavy build-up of cars behind him.

There are troubles on the farm. Morgan's father, now a grand octogenarian, is still called upon to drive the tractor and perform tasks on the farm just when he would have been justified in putting his feet up for life and dreaming old man's dreams in the farmyard, looking over at the blue mountains in the distance.

Even the cows on the farm are discontented. Their tails twitch nervously in the fields, whether or not there are any burdensome flies to perplex them. Their offerings in terms of milk quotas are consistently lower than anywhere else on this green isle and cows have even been seen out in the lanes, thanks to the panoply of holes appearing in badly maintained stone walls and barbed wire fences.

Some of the fields leak cows like water from a colander. Anni, when passing the Davies farm, when Tudur was still a babe in cotton nappies, would sigh at the badly-run decrepit looking farm, and contrast it with her own well-run efficient home.

"Your father would never let his cows roam," she would tell Tudur after his weekly bath when he was lying stretched out before the coal fire, warm and contented, his rubbery limbs shining and clean.

"Cows on the road?" Tudur burbled. "Impossible. Cows don't go on the road."

Hey diddle diddle
the cat and the fiddle
the cow jumped over the moon
. . . la la la
the little dog laughed to see such sport
and the dish ran away with the spoon.

"If the cow can jump over the moon," asserted Anni firmly, "it can certainly go on the road."

She continued combing through his hair with the nit comb.

"And this is more than Morgan Davies will do for his son," she snorted. "Riddled with bugs I shouldn't wonder. You never see him but he's scratching like the fleas are doing a dance on him."

The reason is that nature has not been kind to Morgan's son as it has to Dai's son and heir. The secret is kept as close as the ingredients of a magic potion, but there are nevertheless whispers in the local community about him. It is said that Bryn Davies should be in an institution but that he is only kept from it by the insistence of his father who shows the same suspicion of the medical profession and all offers of help as summer shows towards the Davies family when they attempt to bring the season into its proper place in the calendar. Unless that evasive season were tied effectively to the rear of the powerful tractor, and disallowed any say about whether it follows or not, for sure it would evade its responsibilities and cause havoc by lingering and disrupting the harvest.

In the matter of tying things up it is whispered that Morgan knows more about this than most. It is said that Morgan employs no labourers or outside help on his farm because he does not want outsiders to see what happens to his difficult son at nights.

However it is not my part to spread wicked rumours. We'll have none of that thank you. Thus I will only relate what I know to be true, which is that Morgan Davies never goes to sleep at night without a thick padlock on his bedroom door. And true it is that Bryn always sleeps separately from the rest of the family in a little annexe which only Morgan Davies has the key to. Anyone who was up for morning milking or who took to peeping in at the window, the way first light has a habit of doing, might spot a young man with red marks around his wrists and ankles; and they might spot Morgan Davies putting away some silver

32

implements, which appear to consist of two metal rings, a chain and a key, in a drawer which he locks afterwards.

There was one neighbour of the Davies's, who shall be nameless due to the infamy of his suggestion who, drunk in his cups in the local pub one night, swore that Morgan Davies kept his son handcuffed and bound at nights. He further reported that the bruises Morgan Davies was often seen to sport on market or auction days, were not due to the arduousness of farm work, as he would assert, but that they were due to the kicks and blows dealt by his son as Bryn was led, unwillingly like summer, behind his father in the evenings into his annexe separated from the main house.

In his early school days Bryn resembled nothing so much as a cooked sausage. His socks unfailingly slipped down to his ankles, wrinkled and unappealing like overcooked sausages with wrinkled skins. His school shirt, carelessly hanging out of his trousers, never tucked in, and usually with a button or two missing so that in summer, when he took off his school jumper, you could see pale pink flesh beneath, uncannily resembling the pink meat of an inner sausage when the brown pork cylinders burst their skins through exposure to high heat or not having been pricked carefully with a fork.

Morwena Davies, Bryn's sister, shone at school whereas Bryn was still unable to read or write by the time all of his classmates had mastered those skills. His teachers gave him things to draw which he loved, although he was always extending his artwork from the paper onto his body. He had a habit, when he was seven, of poking his pen through a small hole in his sock, down near the ankle, and scratching, so that whenever he did P.E. in bare feet in the school hall, his ankles resembled nothing so much as notepads, so badly were they scribbled on.

Bryn was also fond of making paper cut-outs, snipping around shapes of animals and then sticking them in collages. Drawing, cutting and sticking were his only interests

33

although the first time he had been given animal shapes and scissors, he had held the cutting implements so close to his attire that he had actually snipped his clothes along with the paper and was forced to go about for the rest of the day dressed in shirt and trousers with cat and dog shaped holes.

He developed one or two odd habits as a child which led to gossip about him. Being an extremely bashful and shy boy he preferred disguising himself or hiding away when he could. He had gone about for some time wearing a stocking on his head which obscured his face and allowed him privacy. His sister's stocking, which looked perfectly respectable when it was on her leg, looked rather peculiar covering Bryn's face, with a little bobble of stocking on the top of his head where the foot should go. As a natural introvert he never could understand why he alarmed people by hiding or lurking about in corners with a stocking on his head.

One of Bryn's favourite pastimes as a child was attempting to catch wild birds. He would set up a trap on the grass with a long length of rope, looped over a tree branch, attached to a milk crate. With the help of some bird food placed under the milk crate, which he held in the air, slightly above the bird seed, by means of the long rope, he hoped to catch some winged creatures. He never succeeded but this hobby nevertheless occupied him for hours at a time.

If you had asked him why he spent so many hours uselessly trying to catch birds, he might disconsolately have answered that he was trying to catch some friends, because Bryn was fond of animals, and he attempted to go about catching human friends in much the same way that he attempted to make avian ones. He had tried several times to kick a football at the head of a boy who showed some friendliness towards him, in the hope that he would injure the boy sufficiently to make him retire from the game and play with Bryn in the playground instead.

When his sister, Morwena, had said, horrified, "Bryn, you can't go about doing things like that. Kicking a ball at Meic's head," Bryn had sorrowfully replied, "I know. I'm not very good at aiming and I might knock someone else out instead of Meic."

The young man never cut his fingernails or his toenails but merely left them until they broke off. Thus he had a mixture of unnaturally long nails intermingled with jagged ones which had broken. The long nails were exceptionally dirty and they had a habit of catching on his bedcovers in the night when he turned over, so that the top sheet was snagged in dozens of places, and his under sheet often felt gritty next to his skin due to a combination of broken dirty nails and biscuit crumbs from the biscuits he liked to eat in bed.

As a teenager Bryn Davies developed a black scowl like hot black coal on the fire. He tattooed the name of his first girlfriend, Ffion Ifans, across his arm when he was fifteen. The tattoo adorning his other arm is to commemorate the year the Davies's barn burnt down. The tattoo on Bryn's shoulder is to mark the year of the burglary. All his life's events mapped out in tattoos. You can read his body like a picture book. One or two livid scars, mainly obscured by the diary of events covering his body, remain.

"What are those scars? Self-harming then?" One of Morwena's friends joked to Bryn. For answer, Bryn turned his shoulder and revealed a knife made of black ink scored into his shoulder blade.

"That's for the time I dropped the knife and sliced my toe."

There was silence for some minutes.

In another country and culture, like Thailand for instance, the decorated boy might have attracted female admirers for his tattooed body, as tattoos are considered something in the nature of amulets or lucky charms offering protection from evil spirits in that country, as well as increasing a person's attractiveness. But illustration of the body not having caught on here in the same way, his effect on his audience was not always what he had hoped for. Neither did his tattoos have the quietening effect on the troublesome Celtic spirits that they have in other places of the world where ghosts and spirits are frightened by tattoos.

Bryn's sister, Morwena, by contrast, was always the neat goody two-shoes; with shoes so highly polished that she could see her face in them when she bent over to admire them, rendering a glance in the mirror unnecessary. Two neat pigtails carefully secured with pristine red ribbons, with the small bows turned infallibly towards the front. Two white socks that never wrinkled nor fell down but stayed inexorably up at the same height, just below two pink scrubbed knees.

Although the seasons may sometimes lag behind time due to the unreliability of human nature, Morwena can always be relied upon to clean her flat on Saturday mornings. She has long lived apart from the family home on Anglesey and removed herself to Bangor on the mainland of Wales, across the stretch of water known as the Menai Strait.

Morwena's best friend, Charlotte, has given up exhorting Morwena to behave as most of the rest of the world does and to go shopping on Saturday mornings. Morwena's response is always along the lines of, "Today I must dust the coving and ceiling corners," or, "This morning I must vacuum along the tops of the picture frames and clean my skirting boards," or sometimes, "Today I must wind the grandfather clock and adjust the weights and wash my tea towels."

Sometimes it seems that Morwena has an unfair advantage in the cleanliness stakes. She rarely allows anyone over the threshold on a Saturday morning so it is a privileged viewer who is able to see what is going on, but I swear that I heard someone who had once been privy to her cleaning mornings, say that her immaculate yellow dusters which always looked as though they had never been used before, sprouted something like a myriad of legs and ran by themselves over the walls and surfaces.

If anyone deserved a medal for friendship it is Charlotte who had been the receptacle of more problems and secrets than the local public house had pulled pints of beer, or nearly so. It was a breach in the levee that let a devastating flood into New Orleans and swept most of that city away; so it is that problems, like water, have periods where they ferment so at the will of nature and freak winds, that they suddenly rise up in a huge surge, overwhelming and devastating.

There have been times when Charlotte has discovered Morwena prostrate and incapacitated, struck with a kind of mental paralysis or depression which leaves her unable to function, to walk to her workplace and perform her role as senior librarian.

Charlotte's mental horizons being well above sea level and rarely subject to sudden and calamitous assaults, she rarely has need to call upon Morwena's resources as a support in times of trouble. This is just as well because on the rare occasions it happened that Charlotte asked for a friendly ear and advice during a time of family trouble, Morwena's response was, "Don't be troubling me for advice; I can hardly cope with my own life."

Due to the nobility of human nature, which is doled out in unequal portions, Charlotte bore her friend no long-term ill will for this callous statement and their friendship was rebuilt after a fashion. Although the old school days when they went about like Siamese twins joined at the arms, and bore similarly coloured ribbons and white socks, were over.

When one child of the family has disappointed, it is natural to look to the rest to recover the family fortunes, thus the burden of expectations on the other child or children are understandably great.

Morwena felt these burdensome expectations more than most. Inherently bright and clever, always impeccably dressed and socially well-behaved, under pressure to conform and rescue her father's flagging hopes of his other offspring, her perception of her duties and responsibilities in that regard might have been seen as exaggerated. Her sense of duty was little less than that of the heir to the throne.

Her promotion to the post of senior librarian within a short period was met with elation by her father, or at least something resembling elation since that was not an emotion readily felt by Mr Davies.

Morwena's relationship with an officer at a nearby RAF base was also a cause for rejoicing with the usually uncommunicative Mr Davies. It seemed so eminently suitable a pairing. And many an RAF young man has ended up with a local Anglesey lass as his wife. However the RAF officer did not ask Morwena to marry him and after three years of friendship it looked less and less likely that he would do so. Morwena tried every indirect means she could think of in order to prompt him into popping the question; every means in short except that of asking him outright. When it became clear that marriage was not going to materialise and the officer finally found someone else, it proved another cause for prostration, misery, and Morwena being unable to get out of bed in the mornings.

Charlotte's suggestion of finding someone else proved to be a double-edged sword. Morwena, intelligent, pretty and with a respectable career, had no trouble in finding someone else, and then someone else, and then someone else after that. Her relationships turned into a desperate search for someone to marry and an interminable and everlasting series of someone else's.

"What is wrong with me?" she would sometimes say to her hairbrush as she brushed out her shiny black hair at night before the looking glass. The glass only reflected her appearance down to her middle, not to her feet, which might have given her a clue to the thing.

It may well be that the root of Morwena's difficulty in finding a soulmate was down to her having cold feet. The Davies family all suffer from the malady of freezing cold feet, and there is nothing so unpleasant as lying next to someone at night with icy feet which do not warm up. Even with two pairs of bed socks, Morwena's pasty ankles always emitted a distinct chill. This was probably due to her grandfather's having been exposed in the snow for several hours not many months after his birth; but this is getting ahead of the story which comes later on in its proper place.

CHAPTER 5

BLUE FLAGS AND RED DRAGONS

List of contents:-

*

I have always considered flags to be something in the nature of toys for boys. This is probably due to the prevalence in my home of little paper flags in jars when I was growing up. My elder and younger brother played something that they called, "Going to war" during our youthful days.

This consisted of opposing armies whose positions were marked by paper flags stuck with pins into a large piece of plywood with rough edges. The plywood overhung the kitchen table when it was allowed to sit up there. Usually my mother would require the table for other purposes however, and then the large piece of plywood would have to sit on the floor.

The flags, I recall, gave great trouble. Due to having been stored furled up in small glass jars, the paper was particularly hard to unfurl and often the flags, which marked the positions of invading armies, would be curled up and require uncurling before it was possible to see which unpleasant nation was doing the invading.

I recall that my brother never wanted to be Ireland because he'd once been sick over the side of the boat going to Ireland. Normally our parents would never have been silly enough to take us across the Irish Sea in January as we were all prone to seasickness, and Rhys more than most children, but the death of a relative in Ireland in January and the necessity of a funeral made it imperative for us to go.

Rhys also had an irrational prejudice against Ireland because, on returning to school after watching our relative's coffin lowered into the frozen ground in Dublin, Rhys's teacher had instructed him to, "Tell the class what *Hibernia* is, Rhys."

And Rhys had answered, "It is the name of the ferry boat going to Ireland."

Rhys's teacher, quite unfairly, sensing cheek, instead of forgiving him a genuine mistake, had moved him from the top table with the clever children to the bottom table for a day; with the result that Rhys had never forgiven Ireland.

The proper place for a flag seems to be on the top of a sandcastle or the flagpole of an ambassadorial residence in a foreign country where it is useful for advertising one's nationality. Or at least it is useful for those unfortunate people who, being persecuted in their own country, want to flee to the embassy of another nation and claim political asylum. The ambassador may not consider himself so lucky or the flag so useful when it attracts the attention of terrorists with a grudge against the embassy's nation, resulting in an attempt to blow it up.

Thanks to the mixed fortunes of flags and their possible inherent dangers, it may seem surprising that flags should be so highly regarded on a small island like Anglesey. However it is flags of the blue variety denoting water quality and not nationality that stir such passions on this small isle.

A blue flag means a highly rated, top quality beach, more visitors and more tourists. I hope it will not seem unpatriotic in the eyes of my fellow islanders to remark that in the competitive race to acquire blue flags and outdo other locations in their acquisition, the islanders may have resorted to cheating. It is as well for me that there is no dedicated bookshop on Anglesey and that my fellow islanders are therefore unlikely to read my report on this because I fear I should come in for more than a few kicks for letting the cat out of the bag.

The truth is that Holyhead, with its already picturesque vista of blue Hibernian sea, white sailed yachts, and long stone breakwater sheltering the harbour and pretty shingle beach, is actually planning to go sandy. In other words, many tonnes of sand, about 15 tonnes in all I am led to believe, are going to be brought in to enhance the already considerable attractions of Newry Beach.

Fearful of the depredations of the sea and the likelihood that the new bought sand might be washed away, it has been planned to deposit the sand carefully above the tideline and shingles, keep it carefully arranged, groomed, brushed and tidied on a weekly basis, and thus steal a march over neighbouring places by boasting not merely a shingle or a sandy beach, but a combined shingle and sand beach.

Of course the report in the newspapers of the spending of so many thousands of pounds for the importation of sand and employing someone to keep it spick and span after its arrival is so much window dressing for those not in the know. It satisfies auditors and WAMs (Welsh Assembly Members) operating at some distance from the isle, but it does not fool the locals who know that the beaches have the ability to arrange themselves to best advantage all around this coast.

The sand having magic powers, with something of the potency of the magic herbs that grow in Anni's garden and which went into the meat pies, has the ability to manicure itself immaculately. Once beach users have gone home at night the beach raises its prone body into a sitting position, shakes itself in the white foam of the incoming tide, and with neat fingers returns each sea creature tidily back into its proper place.

Those early morning risers who like to be up with the sun and on the beach as soon as the tide has started making its journey over to Ireland, catch fleeting glimpses of a retreating sandy form. If they hurried they might have caught sight of a crab being returned to its pool, of the heaps of seaweed being hurriedly swept into piles ready for the sea's last refuse collection before setting off for Ireland. They may have seen a shell turn itself over, displaying itself on its best side, glowing with the desire to be picked off the sand by a child and pocketed for the shell collection.

There have been occasions I am ashamed to report when vast cruise liners have anchored in the deep channel of the port of Holyhead and disgorged their passengers, only to have them bussed off the island for sightseeing in other regions of North Wales. Although not underrating the charms of Conwy and Caernarfon Castles, Bodnant Garden, and Port Meirion, it is nevertheless true that Anglesey has subtle magic properties which disappear at the bridge which joins the isle to the mainland. And it is also true that islanders would prefer the opportunity of seeing the fat purses of cruise line passengers being opened in Anglesey shops rather than elsewhere. And I agree with them.

When it comes to flags the people of Wales are especially tenacious. Not only are they covetous of blue flags which in the bad old days may have caused European nations to go to war, where now they content themselves with banging on the table at Brussels and sniping across diplomatic tables, but they are unmatched in the plethora of red dragons and their ingenuity in finding places from which to drape them. The flags bearing red dragons that is and not red dragons of the fire breathing variety.

The mist that frequently holds this isle in a maternal embrace has another purpose known to locals but carefully kept secret from all outsiders. Like a theatre curtain it conceals the shifting of props and allows no hint of what is happening to come through to the audience. The magical properties of Welsh flags are known only to islanders and so successfully has this secret been kept that when a Welsh flag suddenly appears atop some patently inaccessible place, the off-islander's view of the matter is that young Welshmen are as agile and clever as monkeys in their ability to climb and make themselves invisible at the same time.

The old medieval prophecies that the red dragon shall rise again, however, refer not to the raising of the Welsh dragon on the flagpole, but to the Welsh prince, Owain Glyndŵr, hero of the noble uprising against the English that began around 600 years ago and lasted as long as the Trojan War. Our Welsh hero's flag unfurled against the might of the English army bore the image of a red dragon.

CHAPTER 6

A CHOICE OF DRESSINGS

List of contents:-
Invisible hands keep people indoors.
The island wears a jilbab.
Now it wears a burka.
A breakfast of ducks' eggs; and how the same people always write to the newspaper.
A cow and two smelly pigs.
A bread-making machine and red-bottomed sheep.
Purple lobsters stuffed with secrets.
A choice of dressings for the lobster, and a bad case of indigestion.
Magical gifts conveyed down the line of female Celts.
The Tylwyth Teg – or fairy folk.
Dai wears his underpants in public and shows his old man.

*

Ynys Môn, which stands bracing itself like a shield between Ireland and the north coast of Wales, is constantly under attack from her Hibernian neighbour. Invisible hands creep off the Irish Sea from September onwards, maliciously sweeping tiles from roofs, uprooting trees, overturning garden furniture, keeping the elderly and infirm indoors by pulling hard on the door knockers so that frail hands cannot pull doors open from the inside.

Sometimes the invisible hands tug roguishly at the corners of the sea, lifting the edges like a blanket, peeping underneath, so that the ferries and cargo boats traversing the waters between the two Celtic nations bob and roll like toys toppling from the summit of a hump of blankets when a five year old lifts his knees in bed.

For many of the winter months Anglesey wraps itself in a jilbab with only its face visible, hiding itself from the world. Flashing beacons and lighthouses keep the bobbing toy-like boats from rolling off the grey blanket of sea and off the edges of the world. In the deepest winter the isle adopts the burka, rendering its contours indistinguishable to the outside world. Grey clammy fog adopts a protective posture, carefully bandaging Anglesey in a winter smoke.

Tudur reads the local newspaper each week. Over breakfast of fresh ducks' eggs and newly made bread he always turns to the letters page first. He looks for the names of regular contributors. The chances are, living in such a small community, that he will know the contributors.

I often amuse myself by reading the letters page and attempting to guess who wrote a certain letter, deducing by the style and content who the writer is likely to be before looking at the name. I often wish I had laid a bet on getting the answer right. There is something in particular about a letter of complaint, possibly the clue lies in the tone, that renders a regular contributor easily identifiable from one week to another.

My own nephew told his mother on the phone that, "Aunty Kathryn always buys two newspapers. One has on it *a cow and two smelly pigs*," by which she understood him to mean that I had bought the *Holyhead – Anglesey Mail* as usual. In fact the pigs were not smelly or uncared for as my 6 year old nephew's comments imply. They were in fact prize-winning pigs fast asleep on a bed of straw exhausted from the excitement of the Anglesey Winter Show held annually at the Mona Showground.

On an island not thirty miles across, letters to the editor can punch above their weight. Local rivalries and recriminations take the shape of rain and come hurtling, pelting down, from the skies. It has been said that the rain falls on the just and the unjust alike. And nowhere is this more true than on this little isle safety-pinned to the coast of Wales.

Eiluned, Tudur's new wife, has introduced a bread-making machine. It has precipitated fierce clashes with her mother-in-law, Anni.

"What about proper yeast, kneading and proving?" Anni is aghast at Eiluned's irresponsible new-fangled ways about bread. "Whoever heard of bread without kneading and proving, and rising in a warm place for two hours?"

"It tastes just as good," Eiluned asserts angrily. "You can't tell the difference."

Anni snorts.

"There must be something wrong with it," she contests. "It's not proper bread."

The colour runs into Eiluned's cheeks like sand into the lower chamber of the egg timer. In the space of one minute her cheeks are glowing with an influx of colour like vermilion. Tudur watches the invasion of red dye for a few seconds before hastily excusing himself and heading off for the sheep pastures. He knows he will be safer amongst the red bottomed sheep than with his red-tinged wife at present.

Tudur and Dai's sheep are marked with red dye on their rears for the purposes of identification.

"I wouldn't let anyone put red colour on my bottom," Gwyneth the baby tells Tudur on his way out to the fields. "I'd run away."

"Why do you do it anyway?" Gwyneth asks him accusingly. "Making their bottoms red?"

"It's so we can find them again," Tudur says.

Gwyneth snorts.

She has inherited the snort from Anni. It is the Llewellyn-Jones snort and has been passed down from the ancestors like Anni's milk jug and the solid oak dining table which can seat a dozen grown men or more.

"I wouldn't let you find me by putting red dye on my bottom."

At four years of age, not quite old enough for school, Gwyneth is dependent on her own resources while her siblings are at school or, like Tudur, working on the farm. When the local restaurant owner can be persuaded to allow her some of his time, she likes exploring his sheds at the back of the restaurant where the tanks of water housing live lobsters and crabs are kept. The purple lobsters are hugely fascinating to a small pair of blue eyes. She is sure that their vastness and purple colour is due to their being stuffed with secrets.

It is precisely their being stuffed full of secrets that makes lobsters sometimes hard to digest, I am convinced. One time when I ate a lobster that was bursting at the claws with secrets I was awake for hours at night, groaning and swearing, "I'll never eat another lobster as long as I live."

I don't know what vital secret that lobster was holding onto, but it took a long time for it to pass through my intestines. It was a fortnight at least before I could bring myself to face a lobster again, and next time I made sure I chose a smaller one; a large meal of inedible secrets not agreeing with my digestive system at all.

The biggest purple lobster, bursting out of its shell, is bursting with its own importance and the secrets of the sea. He knows he is a beautiful crustacean though to Gwyneth's eyes his is a horrific, dramatic kind of beauty, closely associated with death and tragedy. Soon that shell will be squealing in the intense heat of a bubbling pot of water on the stove. This, the largest lobster in the store shed, is the most expensive item on the restaurant menu. He comes with a choice of dressings and there is an artistic line drawing of him on the margins of the menu, or possibly one of his large cousins who has already fed the appetite of a diner.

Another pleasurable activity looked forward to whenever her mother or Tudur has time to take her, is paying a visit to the ostrich farm up at Llanfaethlu and watching the big birds with fluffy bedraggled feathers running about their enclosure. The first time Gwyneth saw them she imagined them to be emus, and I rather wish they were since a *mob* of emus is rather more colourfully named than a mere *flock* of ostriches, but ostriches they are, and presumably destined to end as meat on some distant plates since I know of no local pub or restaurant featuring ostrich steaks on its menu.

Gwyneth's other favourite pastime is salvage, retrieving treasure from the sea which has been cast up on the beach. To date there has been an old wooden bookend, stained and mottled by the battering waves, now used to prop up a small line of books on her bedroom windowsill; assorted shapes of coloured glass resembling gemstones which have been worn smooth in the water, and which Gwyneth has put into little metal clasps with necklace chains attached, got from a jewellery making kit which Tudur gave her for Christmas; there is an old anchor in the garden, rendered immovable by small hands due to its size and weight, but Gwyneth had persuaded Tudur to drive the tractor down onto the beach, transport it back to the farmyard and place it in the little patch of earth behind Dai's Christmas trees known as Gwyneth's garden.

It goes without saying that Gwyneth, although the youngest of the Llewellyn-Jones's, had developed the strongest magical capacities. It is a little known fact, found only in the most obscure of Welsh folklore, that magical gifts are sometimes bestowed on the youngest female of a large family; but only where there is an unbroken succession of Welsh blood on both sides of the family and where the female bears the characteristic hallmarks of her Celtic ancestry.

One of the gifts the small girl has been blessed with is the ability to see the Tylwyth Teg – the *fair folk* as they are often known due to their fair colouring – with whom she is almost at eye level, with the fairies perhaps marginally taller. Her father believes that the bowl of milk she takes out at night is for the hedgehogs which have a thoroughfare through the farmyard, but the bowl of creamy milk from the farm cows finds itself placed high up out of reach of those snuffling spiky creatures who shuffle across the grass at night and copulate with squeaks and squeals by the garden fence.

Anni knows better than Dai for, although she has never seen the Tylwyth Teg with her own eyes, she has heard their singing on moonlit nights from the hill above the farm sounding like a watch of nightingales.

All the Llewellyn-Jones's were born with black hair, further blackened with generations of sitting over coal fires on long winter evenings. And Gwyneth has the ocean blue coloured eyes of Welsh children raised looking out at the sea. There is sea, sea, and nothing but sea in all directions on this tiny magical isle with its mysterious rocky contours, its secret herbs and magical plants.

The mushrooms spring up overnight. Gwyneth gathers them in the front pocket of her pinafore, the hood of her cardigan, and her green toy wheelbarrow and takes them to her mother.

"Mushrooms for breakfast, Mam."

Anni fries them, heating the skillet until it smokes and shaking the mushrooms back and forth. They go straight into the pan as nature intended, without washing, and with small lumps of earth clinging to their undersides.

As everyone knows who has eaten fresh mushrooms straight from the field for breakfast, cooked in butter, each plate of mushrooms is given its distinctive flavour from the variety of earth clinging to the fungus umbrella. Mother and daughter can differentiate the different kinds of earth and would know immediately, without being told, from which part of the land the mushrooms had been gathered. Anni knew without asking Gwyneth that they came from the field next to the milking sheds, and not from the field by the church or from along the edges of the driveway.

Since his stroke Dai has become forgetful, his memory has become like an old leaking milk bucket. The mirror in his bedroom is positioned so that it only reflects his torso above the waist. Dai frequently forgets to put on his trousers and wanders down to breakfast and sometimes into the garden in his underpants. The Catholic priest often calls to see him, to offer him the consolations of religion in his final years. He calls one afternoon when Dai is sitting reading the newspaper in the garden in his underpants.

"Hey Tudur," Huw mutters to his brother. "Dad's only wearing underpants. He's showing his old man. He can't go about doing that."

"It's lucky that the priest came today then," Tudur says loftily. "Because when you're at school and Dad sits indoors watching television he doesn't even bother with the underpants."

The priest is embarrassed. His dreams are all about undergarments. He cannot escape them. Pants escape from his dreams and into his waking hours. They take cover behind apparently benign items of furniture or in the hidden recesses of his own home and then taunt him by appearing like mystical visions, unseen by other people. Like the holy children of Fatima or the Lourdes visionary, he experiences visions of things invisible to others. The shame and embarrassment of seeing things that remain unseen by his friends, and the souls he ministers to, constitute his own personal hair shirt.

To escape the company of disturbing visions, and dreams that become solid, he takes to going out. His life is a round of visits. Round and round on the roundabout without ceasing he visits one parishioner after another. When he has to sit alone in his house next to the church he becomes morose and desperate.

He is glad to visit Dai and leave the mocking, laughing whispers that speak out of dusty corners in his presbytery and church. But he is horrified by Dai's underpants. Bright

51

blue Simpson pants, a replica of those in his dreams. They were Tudur's idea of a joke present for Dai last Christmas. Dai has never worn them until now, when his mind began to leak like that old milking pail he can't bring himself to throw away because it was used on the farm when his own grandfather was farming. Dai himself used to follow his grandfather and father around the farm just as Gwyneth follows Dai and Tudur around now.

CHAPTER 7

ANGELS AND ROOSTERS

List of contents:-

*

If Dai's farm is held up as a model of efficiency and good management, like a well-run factory production line, Anni's brother's farm is exactly the opposite. Between Anni's husband and brother and their other farming relatives, they own enough farmland to create a dynasty but Wyn is letting the side down.

His farmhouse is badly situated. According to ancient and respected oriental wisdom, if your house is situated inauspiciously on a river, on the wrong side of a bend for example, the good luck carried along by the river will miss your bank and hit the other one or simply roll straight past.

Wyn's farm was the equivalent of a house built on the wrong side of a river bend. The luck just carried on past his farm and went straight down the track to Dai and Anni's place. The Celtic spirits of the land were definitely against Wyn. Once you have turned the spirits of the land against you, it is curtains for you. Seven generations a curse on the land lasts, and there's no way of ridding yourself of it, except by such extremes of penance that you may as well begin by burning the land and starting again from scratch.

Wyn is famed for his parties. The amount of wine and beer consumed in his farmhouse is legendary. It is said by those in the know that the partygoers arrive with the onset of dusk and don't leave until daylight. The last guests are to be found with their heads on the hearth long after the coal fire has gone out. Those guests lying sprawled around the field amidst the trestle tables and the remains of food left out to the air and insect life all night, wake to headaches, benumbed limbs and the sound of the rooster crowing.

I cannot tell you where in the line of succession this rooster comes because there have been so many that I have lost count. Each one has fallen victim to Wyn's colossal hangovers and his black cauldron of a temper which simmers and bubbles when he's in his drink so that he grabs the nearest thing he can and wrings its neck.

By first light the cows are coming down from the gorse hillside where they have sheltered for the night and are beginning to nose at the patches of grass and vomit. Wyn, known as mad Wyn in the locality, confirms his mad reputation by leaping from the dewy field into the kitchen as though he'd been fired from a gun, swearing that he'd seen a black and white apparition floating above him as he lay on his back in a drunken stupor, which he'd taken to be a vision of angels.

The soft black and white muzzles of the bovine creatures picking their way amongst the litter of bodies, torn tablecloths, empty wine bottles, tattered party banners and streamers, are far from his mind this morning.

A murder of crows gathers to scavenge what scraps they can from Wyn's lawn. To my mind, crows are a most sinister looking bird, with their hooded night black eyes and funereal cawing. On the first occasion I heard a group of crows referred to as a *murder* it immediately struck me as an appropriate term for such an evil visaged set of birds.

In the early light of dawn when even cursed places catch a ray of sunshine, the barely visible strands of good luck which run down the hill show like rainbow arcs. Wyn is too busy to notice that one end of the rainbow begins above him up the hill, arches over his place, and that the other end of the rainbow falls effortlessly into Anni's herb garden on the next farm.

Anni sees the rainbow of light falling into her garden through the kitchen window and sighs. She does not talk about the little people with anyone; people hereabouts know that fairy favour and the good luck brought by the Tylwyth Teg is not to be talked of. But she knows like all the wise women of ancient stock on this isle that her brother has invited the wrath of the small people with his slovenly ways. The Tylwyth Teg are scrupulously clean people and taunt and tease the inhabitants of dirty houses until they are like to run mad.

There are many nights that Wyn does not go to sleep until first light is breaking. If sleeping is the right word. He hardly sleeps at all. The drinking would go on long into the night. Many times of an early morning he fell asleep fully clothed, lying belly down, face turned to one side so he could breathe. Often there was barely a minute before walking unsteadily from the door and collapsing on the bed and entering deep sleep for only a couple of hours.

The bed sheets in the room that Wyn slept in never got changed. They were covered in food, coffee and whisky stains. Plates and cups got taken to his room and ended up in heaps, dirty, and never taken to the kitchen unless his wife did it. But the stubborn old man refused to let his wife change the bedclothes; he said he preferred the natural body smells that God had given him and that he hated the feel of freshly laundered sheets as they were too cold to sleep in.

There was a story put about by Glynn Hughes in the pub one night that Salie, Wyn's wife, stripped the bed of its sheets every six weeks and either put them in the bin or burnt them. But Gwyneth, who heard about the story from Tudur, knew better.

"It's the Tylwyth Teg, isn't it?" She consulted the farm cats because it would have been impolite to talk to her mother about the fairies. "They don't like Uncle Wyn's dirty house, and they come and take his bedding away."

For those sceptics who prefer a more rational explanation for the missing bedding, and suspect Wyn's wife of duplicity in the matter, it should be said in her defence that no one had ever found any remnants of cloth in the farm incinerator or in the dustbin which Wyn regularly checked before it was taken away by the council refuse collection truck. In the absence of evidence, it seems a more plausible explanation to suspect the Tylwyth Teg who are known for their thieving and mischievousness, and their hatred of sloppy housekeeping. The fact of the bedding disappearing so thoroughly without a trace lends itself to come magical explanation since the fairy folk are well known for removing things, including children on occasion, without trace.

The coloured lights adorning Wyn's house are still alight at 6 am, though no longer blazing as they had the evening before. Many of them have been broken during the revels of the night. Mad Wyn and Glynn Hughes had lain on their backs the previous evening, aiming wine corks at the light bulbs, leaving jagged edges of glass dangling from the wires and shattered fragments along the gravel paths.

While many of the insalubrious ragtag of revellers limp wearily home in company with the dawn, some of them to set about a day's work, some of them to bed, Wyn drives his tractor straight down through the fields. Wyn owns most of the land hereabouts. The largeness of his expanse makes him contemptuous of the forms and authorities lying outside it.

Wyn has been running foul of the authorities for years. Planning laws he holds in small regard. A range of outhouses, garages, sheds, stables, have grown up piecemeal on his land, a tribute to the feelings of one man who believes it is his right to do exactly as he pleases on his own land.

Trouble rises out of the ground for Wyn as crane flies — Daddy long legs to you and me — rise out of the ground in August and September. Trouble starts out small like the grub in the ground, inching its way out of the earth, but when it emerges it has six enormous legs and a pair of wings to fly with too. Wyn's troubles always have wings to fly with, and there is a bumper crop both of crane flies and troubles this year.

He sets off in his tractor at breakneck speed. All is well while the tractor is rattling over the turf of his own place, but when he hits the public highway, which splits part of his land in two; those flying troubles come buzzing round him with so many long legs you wouldn't believe. The tractor overturns in the ditch on the highway and the authorities are down on Wyn before you can say, "Rabbit pie."

Those of us who have lived on this magic island for many years know that nothing is coincidence and nothing is unplanned. Bad luck? Good luck? It comes for a reason. All part of the wisdom of the land and what goes around comes around.

Wyn had been venting his feelings for the authorities and for the planning laws for a while. They constantly pestered him about the state of his land. His farmhouse, standing in an uneven, tattered line of bits and pieces of buildings along the track is an eyesore. His huge bales of hay are stacked up around his farmyard longer than any other farmer's; and the vast green bags he wraps them in can be seen for miles around. Wyn's irritation about what he could do on his own land took vent in a huge compost heap which he built in full view of the road. And as the filthy heap grew higher and more smelly, his irritation, rather than subsiding, grew with it.

There was a paranoia about Wyn's place among the locals. Those who lived in the little village clustered round the windmill viewed his outrageous palace of pleasure perched above them on the hillside with disdain and suspicion. His revelling was viewed in the light of the sin of Sodom and Gomorrah and it was prophesied that it would all come to no good.

The no good came sooner than anyone had expected. For most of the immediate family the news came down the telephone wire. For the rest of us, the news was gleaned from the local newspapers.

Anni had a hint of what was to come while she sat brushing her hair at bedtime before the window that overlooked Wyn's farmland. Down through the fields came a bright bluish light that failed to flicker as a normal candle would. But a candle it was. Troubled, Anni drew her curtains. Her mother and grandmother before her had told her the stories of phantoms funerals and death candles carried by the pygmy race who live under barrows, mounds and lakes, and how they precede a real death.

Whenever her brother's kitchen fire was unlit she knew he filled it with prickly gorse or sometimes with a box of sharp knives; an old remedy for keeping the fairies out of the house once their ill will has been incurred. Nightly he lay thorns or prickles behind the front and back doors once he had locked them. The Tylwyth Teg are said to be deterred by anything sharp placed in front of an entrance. But the many nights he got drunk in the summer and fell asleep sozzled on the grass, leaving the doors wide open for partygoers, also allowed entry for the indignant small folk.

"My God," said Tudur when he saw the pages of the newspaper. "Will you look at that."

"Why is Aunt Salie in the newspaper?" Rhodri asked over the duck eggs and fresh hot bread.

But Aunt Salie was nowhere. All that was left of Aunt Salie was a black and white photograph in the local newspaper under the heading of *Police Investigation*.

As anyone who has ever been hunting knows, rumours are notoriously hard to shoot. Rabbits, pheasants, foxes, easy by comparison. Few people have seen the rumour bird close up and reported sightings are contradictory, but there are some who say rumours wear camouflage feathers to make themselves indistinguishable from the landscape. Whether this is true or not, two facts are indisputably true. It is recorded in one of those old books of folklore, which my great grandmother had sitting on her mantelpiece, that the rumour bird is fleet of wing and that no one has ever succeeded in shooting one.

Leaving aside the story of Deiniol Cadwallader, who is supposed to have come closer than anyone else to shooting a rumour bird, no one has yet come close to capturing one of these birds. Notoriously truthful as Deiniol is, I have no reason to suspect him of deviating from the truth on the occasion when he averred that he once caught the wing of one of these elusive birds with his shotgun and that, wounded, with only one good wing, it nevertheless continued to rise and fall above the landscape, attempting to fly yet skimming the ground with its now unbalanced wings, leaving blood stains at intervals on the earth. It is possible that rumour birds just vanish into the earth when they are shot, for sure no one has yet been able to display the trophy of a fully feathered rumour bird on their wall.

Aunt Salie was now gone like the rumour bird into the earth. But her demise left a black simmering pot of suspicion and a police investigation. It was known that Wyn had turned his fists on his wife in the past after he'd come back full as a vat of wine from the local pub, and that she'd sported bruises here and there on her body after one of Wyn's particularly vicious hangovers; but this time the papers were talking about possible murder. Analogies were drawn with roosters and wrung necks. Salie had been found with a broken neck at the foot of the stairs.

Anni remained true to her flesh and blood. "I know he's a baddun at times," she insisted to Tudur, "but he's still my flesh and blood, true Celtic blood and Welsh language on both sides, and there's no way he'd kill his wife. He was fond of Salie. We all were. It'll be those bad eyes of hers."

The stories left behind by the rumour bird as it alighted here and there were of quarrels and pushing and a fatal shove down the stairs.

Anni and the other Llewellyn-Jones's stuck to their guns about Salie's short-sightedness and an accidental fall down the stairs resulting in a broken neck. The police investigation continued but Wyn's smelling, putrid heap of compost was suddenly arrested in its growth. Everything came to a stop: the green plastic covered bales of hay, the speeding tractor, and the parties. When Lot's wife looked back at Sodom in the midst of its revels, all unsuspecting of the destruction about to be unleashed on its city walls, she was turned into a pillar of salt. Wyn's wife was now salt of a kind. Dust of the earth.

CHAPTER 8

PHYSICIAN HEAL THYSELF

List of contents:-

*

Trouble arrived in Porth Swtan, the place about which everybody says, "Where's that then?" Until you tell them that the Lobster Pot restaurant is down in the bay and then of course everyone knows instantly where Porth Swtan is.

The trouble arrived replete with beer and sandwiches on the train from South Wales in the form of seven new immigrants from Cardiff, therefore one trouble for every day of the week. Despite bearing the surname common to vast numbers of Welsh men and women, these Jones's appear to have lost their roots. At least that is what they told people. They had moved to North Wales in order to recover their roots which had somehow gone missing during their years

61

living in the Welsh capital and also in Shropshire just over the border from Wales.

It is a well-known fact about Shropshire that it is a place whose citizens are always moving on; a place with a population constantly in flux. It is as though it has suffered some difficulty in choosing its allegiance, placed right on the border there of England and Wales, with a large number of Welsh inhabitants.

Certainly it is also true that I am regularly plagued by unsolicited emails from an estate agent in that part of the world who is determined to replace Shropshire's evacuees with equal numbers of new residents. So enthusiastic is he in his profession that he regularly bombards my computer, and those of others who have absolutely no intention of moving house in the foreseeable future, with house particulars.

Even the SPAM filter is unable to weed out this particularly persistent seller of houses. How it is that he slips through into my inbox uninvited and unwanted, and in spite of my clicking the mouse on the box that says, *block this sender*, I cannot say. For persistence and ingenuity in his determination to sell houses in Shropshire he is to be commended; but his persistence in targeting me I can only regret.

Mrs Jones from both Cardiff and Shropshire, was vehemently indignant about her roots. Her constant theme that they were missing due to the iniquity of the English and not being allowed to speak Welsh at school in the bad old days, when the best that many Welsh citizens could do was to learn their own language out of a book like French or German and possibly pass an 'O' Level in it, was such a source of irritation to her that she had developed ulcers and other ailments as a form of protest.

Mrs Jones had failed the Welsh 'O' Level. Her written performance was not up to the pass standard of the time, but neither was her written English either so that, in fact, her abilities in the imposed language did not surpass her abilities in her native one. Mrs Jones had grown up learning the kind of pure Welsh for passing examinations that is of absolutely no use at all if one has a desire for communication with other people.

The fact is, no one could understand her Cardiff style of school Welsh in the local shop, or in the coffee shops of North Wales where her peers gathered to gossip over deeds and events in the community. Mrs Jones had grown cantankerous and sour about the disadvantages she laboured under, all due to the English, and she had persuaded her husband to move to North Wales with the aim of recovering her lost Welsh roots about which she had been reading, and learning to speak Welsh in a way that would mean she could at last hold a conversation in her own language.

Although strictly speaking, these Jones's should be known as the Cardiff/Shropshire Jones's, it would seem churlish to hold against them the fact that they had been living in Shropshire, foreign country, for so long. After all, they are the right side of the border now. They have not the distinguished pedigree of the Rhydwyn-Jones's for example or the Rhys-Jones's, having mixed blood with foreigners in Shropshire somewhere along the way but, nevertheless, they deserve the dignity of being known as the Cardiff-Jones's.

The Cardiff-Jones's then, moved into the barn house near the church. They were renting the house from Morgan Davies who said, when his curious neighbours asked him about the building and what he was doing with it since they had never seen him carry out repairs before, "If I can rent it out, it's a converted barn; if no one wants it, it's a cowshed."

Myfanwy, better known as Mivvy Cardiff-Jones, was a stick-thin little waif who regularly threatened to throw herself out of the bedroom window which overlooked the garden. It is a very pleasant garden, as Morgan Davies's pigs and his tumbledown sheds are well out of sight. There is a green hosepipe and pretty flowers including sea pinks, and echium spreading itself out in the flower beds like an uninvited relative reluctant to return home.

The lawn is being eaten away by pretty purple flowers which are only pretty and purple for part of the year and are weeds really. But Mrs Cardiff-Jones will not allow them to be removed in the interests of the lawn and there they go, growing wilder and wilder.

Mivvy's doctor avers that she is likely to die of starvation if the fall out of the bedroom window does not kill her first. She is under regular analysis because, as the doctor said sternly to her angry, protesting mother, "Mivvy seems not to be sure where her next meal is coming from, and indeed whether it will ever arrive at all."

The eldest Cardiff-Jones child is Lara whose bibulous habits are becoming notorious in the locality. Her favourite drink is pink champagne and on hot summer days she will not hear of consuming it without strawberries. The strawberries have to be on the table in bowls and in the champagne cut up.

Once, when she had a new boyfriend, Lara bought pearls to put in the champagne instead of strawberries.

"This," she said to her siblings, "is the thing to do."

Although when I mentioned it to my partner, Martyn, the vicar's son, he seemed to think it was an incomprehensible and pointless thing to do. At that specific moment in time I was left with a mystified sense that life was passing by me misunderstood. I have no doubt that it would all make sense if I were only cleverer or had paid greater attention at school. But that is rather too late now.

When Lara shouts she does not just shout, she screams very piercingly. The neighbours then know all her business because her voice is audible from the top of the hill by the architect and his wife, down to the sea's edge. When Wyn was up-ending himself like a duck over the pub wall and turning out the contents of his stomach one or two nights in a row, in his drunken stupor he thought himself to be hearing a television set with the volume turned up.

I have always had sympathy for anyone with car trouble seeing that these coloured boxes of metal on wheels are indispensable for country living. There is no member of the community here who is not dependent on a car; that is, dependent either on owning their own, or on someone else owning a car and being prepared to drive them about if they are too young, or too elderly and frail to hold a licence themselves.

Sometimes the Cardiff-Jones's public-spirited neighbours have complained to the authorities that two of the family's cars parked outside have out-of-date tax discs, thus encouraging a greater degree of noise from that family, several members of whom have screamed at the unimpeachable citizens who have taken on the duty of policing the local community in view of the shortage of uniformed officers in the district.

Ioan Cardiff-Jones, the eldest son, also owns a canary yellow coloured double-decker bus which he parks in the lay-by outside the garden. Certain neighbours, complaining of, "A banana coloured eyesore," have attempted to have the bus removed on the grounds that it requires a special permit to park a bus and that it should attract a parking fee.

Ioan defends it stoutly, insisting that it is a private vehicle, not in public service (despite sometimes being opened for large noisy parties), therefore he should be allowed to park it on the highway at no extra charge. He spends his weekends cleaning off the graffiti the bus has acquired and the rude names sprayed across its rear by local ruffians.

Whether the double-decker fulfils road safety criteria I could not tell you, buses being difficult and expensive to get through the MOT, but it has served Ioan well as a private and enclosed travelling venue for parties since there is such irrational prejudice in the community at large about boomboxes and alcohol and yellow buses and the odd cannabis joint.

The Cardiff-Jones's are an interesting family if not very stable, according to Mivvy's analyst, Doctor Hughes. Dr Hughes's alarm about the family was justifiably increased when his own grown-up daughter began seeing the eldest Cardiff-Jones son, Ioan.

"Don't get in the bus with him," he instructed his daughter, Anwen. "It's far too risky. Just meet him neutrally if you must go out with him. But don't pay him visits at home. That family spells trouble with a capital T."

As Dr Hughes had not been present when the figure of Trouble got off the Cardiff train with the Jones's, mingling with the family and dressed in an anonymous suit, this was rather unfair of him. The phrase *physician heal thyself* springs to mind at this point. Dr Hughes's own son, severely troubled with paranoid schizophrenia, was unwelcome in a number of houses in the neighbourhood. When it became known that Eirian the lawyer's husband was regularly going shooting with Aled Hughes, the doctor's son, and even lending him a gun, there was consternation from the top of the hill right down to the bottom.

Eirian, already chastened from nearly making heads roll in the sea with the kayak, in the manner of the French guillotine, and not minded to get into any more dangerous sports, is furious with her husband for lending Aled Hughes the gun.

"Have you a brain in your head?" she rages at him. "Are you a solid thinking Welshman or not? To be giving a gun to a lad who forgets his medication five days of the week. And who'll be defending you in court if he ends up shooting a body? Not me for sure."

There is something in the quality of the magic air around this isle that ensures the efficient spread of communications. Whatever is uttered, even in the privacy of one's own home to one's nearest and dearest, is sure to be carried on the air and to find its way by some obscure current to other farms and cottages.

Like the rumour bird, the gossip spider is notoriously shy. Only one or two people in any generation are fortunate enough to see its shadowy presence in some neglected ceiling corner or unswept crevice around the edges of a floor. It scuttles, shy of the light, from dark shadow to dark shadow and has a habit of camouflaging itself so effectively that even if, by some remote chance, you heard the barely audible sound of eight spidery legs creeping in some dusty corner, by the time you had fetched a light or candle to illuminate it, it would be long gone.

If the Post Office could deliver letters and parcels across this isle with the efficiency that the gossip spider can disseminate myths and tales via its invisible airborne network of thread, the profits of the Post Office would set it beyond any threat from competitors or private courier firms. Alas, the speed of the spidery silk vine is matchless.

It took so little time for Eirian's remark to be carried on the wind, via a complicated route of crofts and dwellings, that before you could say *Tylwyth Teg*, her words had metamorphosed into a tiny creature with eight legs that was inching its way down through the Hughes's chimney and in at the ears of Dr Hughes. The doctor had each and every medical skill that medical school and training could give him; but he lacked one skill which would have helped him to translate Eirian's remarks in the spirit in which they were thrown on the wind. He lacked the power of analogy.

Dr Hughes's remarks about the inadvisability of travelling in buses with the Cardiff-Jones family had already made their way in at a convenient orifice on the Cardiff-Jones home. Finding the chimney ablaze with the good coal fire that burned in the grate at the Cardiff-Jones's barn house, the implacable spider had tried a few doors and windows. Finding each temporarily closed, it had tried the air bricks instead, quickly finding entry at ground level and settling itself quietly on the kitchen ceiling just next to an old wooden beam of extremely dark wood where its spidery limbs matched the wood. There it sat unseen and untroubled, but with a wide perspective on the life going on below which it observed upside down, its feet being glued to the ceiling for safety.

Dr Hughes, poor man, was merely uttering the truth as he saw it. He intended no malice in his remarks but his failure of analogy, to acknowledge the thin spidery strings of connection that ran between his son's treatment in the community and his own attitude to the Cardiff-Jones's led to him being labelled a hypocrite and to his daughter Anwen moving out of the house and into the Cardiff-Jones's house to live with Ioan the eldest son. Banned from that family's bus, Anwen took refuge in their house instead.

Poor Doctor Hughes was thus afflicted on two fronts. First in the loss of his daughter Anwen to the most unstable family in the neighbourhood, and also by the ill temper of his son Aled who, deprived of his shooting practice with Eirian's husband, took instead to shooting and sniping verbally at his father.

He proved to be as good a verbal shot as he was at aiming for rabbits and pheasants with the gun and in only a month or two the doctor was wishing that he could put a padlock on his door the way it was rumoured that the Davies's doors were padlocked. Unfortunately Dr Hughes had an unimpeachable medical record and was unable to stoop down to standards of medical care for his son that were rumoured to take place elsewhere. He was forced to put up with dissension in the ranks where his own home was concerned.

As for Eirian the lawyer, her misfortunes were multiplying at the rate of Hydra's heads. No sooner had one menace been dealt with then more sprang up to take its place. Having nearly decapitated a number of the bay's denizens with her canoe and having her shouts of remorse and alarm transposed by the wind into insults about, "Fat arses," her private remarks to her husband about Aled Hughes were also stirred by the wind, spiced up and made inflammatory, like adding ginger and cayenne pepper to a bland dish, with the consequence that she was regularly subjected to unpleasant social experiences.

In Lewis Carroll's story it is the Cheshire cat's body that disappears leaving its smile. In Dr Hughes's case it was his smile that disappeared and his body that remained. Eirian's presence on any occasion, whether it was in the local shop, the restaurant, the lay-by for pulling into on the single track road, or some more distinguished social occasion for bay citizens, began unfailingly to induce the strange Cheshire cat phenomenon in reverse.

An additional misfortune was that Eirian and Dr Hughes had previously had friends and acquaintances in common and these friends found the body without a smile a curiously embarrassing experience. One or two people began to turn their backs on Eirian in order to look more directly in Dr Hughes's face, hoping to encourage the smile to resume its place on top of his shoulders.

There were some who attributed Eirian's new found unpopularity to the empty bottles of Chateau Lafite she put on view, by the community recycling bin, for the neighbourhood to see, instead of placing them in the box and closing the lid as everyone else did, but I suspect this to be mere jealous gossip from those acquaintances less clever and less rich than the talented lawyer who were envious of her Porsche boxster.

"It's not bloody fair," Eirian would rail furiously at her husband in the privacy of their bedroom at night. Being a lawyer she considered justice and fairness to be part of her remit, something she was engaged with continuously in her professional life and therefore something at which she should have a definite advantage. To be the victim of injustice was rankling to the spirit of the lawyer.

It is a mark of Eirian's sterling character that she is an utter perfectionist. In her career at Bodedern School, before being beckoned to Oxford for her law degree, she had been known for her competitive spirit. In the 100 metre sprint on sports day she had attracted more attention for her second place in the race than the winner had for gaining first place. Her blue ribbon for coming second had been thrown back at the innocuous seeming helper who had tried to pin it on her school sports shirt, because, "I didn't come first and I should have done. I don't want second."

Eirian's commendable desire always to excel was occasionally undermined by the attitude of lesser mortals who were willing to settle for humbler achievements and prizes in life. Her husband was entirely willing to settle for a lower salary than Eirian's considerable one, and to give her precedence on any social occasion, and to do the school run and baby-sitting when her career demanded it, or when her presence at law functions, lawyers' balls or social events required it. Dr Hughes was not nearly so obliging, refusing to bow down to the prodigious talent before him.

Eirian was as infuriated by the good doctor's attitude as she was when some bombastic or recalcitrant judge refused to recognise the merits of her client's case and awarded it to the other side. On these occasions her face would glow as black as her dark Welsh hair.

"Stupid chauvinist," she had been known to mutter under her breath. "Prejudiced bastard. He just doesn't like women." Or, if the Judge was English, "He just doesn't like the Welsh."

.

CHAPTER 9

KNIVES, FORKS AND
PARKING FINES

List of contents:-
The largest collection of parking fines in North Wales.
The bailiffs are always coming.
The difficulties of mixing only with deep people.
The joys of loft-living but don't forget to close the window in the roof.
A well-aimed peck is all you can expect.

*

Another affliction troubling the Cardiff-Jones family, as if they did not have enough troubles, is that the bailiffs are always coming. The good fortune that three family members have names with the same initial has saved many a car and stereo from being seized by bailiffs confused as to whose property they were seizing. Lara has the largest collection of parking fines in North Wales. She puts them in the glove compartment to hide them from her father who is ferocious about her lapses and she cannot be putting up with his temper about them because they are so numerous.

When they start falling out of the glove compartment, they get transferred to the drawer under the computer but this is the place for many other documents that would otherwise be lost and so they are often found there by her father. To avoid this she puts them in her underwear drawer where they are never found and when they get too numerous amongst her lace and satin she puts them in the wastepaper basket in her bedroom. The bedroom next to the one that Mivvy always says she is going to throw herself out of but never does.

Mivvy went so far as to hang out a long way so that her mother, sitting in the garden amongst the flowers and the hosepipe, had to run upstairs pretty smartly and pull her back. I think this happened rather often, at least according to her elder sister Lara who keeps the record of such things.

You cannot be in Lara's club of nice people if you disagree with her and that would be a heavy blow because she mainly decides for the rest of the family who are the nice people. As she is always right I would not dare to dispute this point with her.

The Hughes family, apart from Anwen who is sharing what used to be the old barn loft with Ioan, have been relegated to the category of *idiots*, and therefore fit subject matter for mealtime banter with which Anwen willingly joins in, except for the moments when she goes out to the kitchen to get spoons because Mrs Jones and Lara never remember to put enough serving spoons on the table. So if she didn't want the yoghurt mixed up with the cous cous or the French dressing, or the olives with the homous, then she had to bring the spoons herself.

Anwen had tried, like a dutiful daughter, to abide by her father and mother's wishes in only bringing "deep" people back home and not "shallow" ones. But she had often not succeeded, not having the unerring judgement of character that life experience and medical practice had given to her father. Once she had brought someone in trouble back home who was only a little bit drunk, and not out of the ordinary way drunk, and she was accused of being "shallow" herself and selfishly taking up the sitting room when Mrs Hughes was needing to hang the new curtains and put on the new cushion covers which the guest was getting in the way of.

Freed from inhibition concerning the use of the correct knives, forks, and numbers of serving spoons, as well as the onerous responsibility of only mixing with deep people, Anwen settled in with the Cardiff-Jones's.

72

It would be very useful if people could be branded on their foreheads as sheep and cattle are branded on their rumps, taking all the bother out of assessing them for oneself. It would save a great deal of trouble and failure in life, guaranteeing sound relationships and connections without any effort at all. However this paradisiacal state of affairs does not exist and we must give up lamenting that it doesn't, and say that Anwen was feeling considerably happier with the Cardiff-Jones's than she had at home under the more exacting standards of Dr Hughes.

It may be that living in a loft was something to do with the cause of Anwen Hughes's happiness. There is nothing as cosy as a loft to live in; high above the tree tops, if there had been any trees in this magnificent spot by the Cardiff-Jones's home, which there are not, unfortunately, because it is too windswept.

However, there are splendid views from the loft window which is flush with the sloping roof. If there had been a bay window, the situation would have been ideal because there is nothing like a seat in a bay window overlooking the sea for lifting the spirits. To get the views from the Cardiff-Jones's loft you have to stand on the bed, crane your neck upwards and press your nose against the window to see out, unless one prefers sky views. All one needs for a view of sky and clouds is to lie back on the bed and look upwards, and there is a perfect square of blue sky, or red sky, or black sky, or grey sky, or whatever colour it happens to be, all year round.

If one is tall enough or able to manoeuvre a box onto the bed for elevation, it is possible to open the loft window wide enough to stick out one's head and enjoy a splendid panorama of waves tipped with foam, fields of grass and sheep, and plenty of scrub, gorse and rocky outcrop. But this is not possible in winter when the wind can almost take one's head off at that height, and when the rain falls straight down through the open window onto the bed. Mrs Cardiff-

73

Jones has already replaced one mattress due to Ioan forgetting to close the window before he went off for the weekend and the rain falling in, causing a soggy and smelly square patch of yuk to develop on the bed below.

The wet soaked straight through the bedclothes to the mattress underneath in a square shape. The bed was so wet that it refused to dry and the stink of mould and mildew led Mrs Jones to call for a special collection from the refuse collection department because she could not bear the stink of rained-on mattress.

There have been one or two other disagreeable happenings in the loft, such as a swarm of bees taking up residence in there, and Ioan receiving about 15 stings in one go due to not having proper bee clothing. It is disconcerting how those bees can get in at any gap or crevice in your jacket and trousers, and into places you wouldn't quite expect.

And then there was the slate that slipped out of place in the wind and the two seagulls that moved into the loft through the gap in the tiles before it could be fixed. It is surprising how aggressive two squatting seagulls can be who have decided to become tenants without your permission. They care nothing for landlord's rights or rent books or any such things. A well-aimed peck is all you can expect if you try to evict seagulls without proper protection.

But these were all minor mishaps, not reflecting the pleasures of living high up, above everyone else. In general for tranquillity and peace, warmth and comfort, a well-insulated loft is hard to beat as a living space.

CHAPTER 10

THE HEDDLU

List of contents:-

*

According to Lara there are many fearsome words in the Welsh language, especially the very many containing double consonants, but none more so than the word HEDDLU. Seen, as it usually was, through the rear view mirror of her car, stamped in black letters across the bonnet of the big white Land Rover immediately behind, or seen in hot pursuit of villains, criminals, or hapless motorists, it was even more fearsome. It bore no relation to the English word p*olice* and the intimidating H at the beginning and two DDs in the middle inspired fear in the heart of some people as it would if the word was spelt *Hoodlum*.

Lara had learned to read the word backwards through the mirror instantly and to understand its meaning, even though she was one of those incompetent language learners who could learn whole long lists of foreign words without ever learning how to string them together. Unlike her mother Mrs Jones, Lara was not in the least concerned with her roots, absent or otherwise, but the sight of a white vehicle with lights on top in the car mirror elicited sensations of anxiety and she was ready with previously formulated excuses.

"I sneezed. It made me temporarily lose control of my car and appear to weave from side to side along the A5025 there. I've been reversing police officer, I'll fasten the seat belt again immediately."

The chief constable's promise to wage war on the speeding drivers of North Wales has left her with an unconquerable fear of and aversion to the *Heddlu*, seeing them not as friends to law and order, the ones who allow her to lie safe in her bed at night, but as vile designing tricksters, lurking in every side road, triumphant when they caught her at five miles over the speed limit enroute to the Thai takeaway at Valley on a Saturday night.

Or at least that is the rendezvous place cited by Lara when asked her destination by the police officer. In fact the real location of her intent was the public house within a short distance of the takeaway premises, but it seemed impolitic to mention this to the officious police officer who was requiring her to, "Blow into this plastic bag, Madam," and instructing her to produce her driving licence and car insurance documents at the police station within ten days.

On arrival at the pub, however, her suggestion of abandoning the car in the car park for the night and walking to the bus stop for the return journey met with incredulity from her comrades in the public house.

"Walking!" Theo said, for it was none other than the architect's son, Theo Williams, grimacing.

"Nuts!" said Glyn.

"You mean something like what Wordsworth did with his sister?" said Theo, for he had achieved an education, though he tried his best to disown it. "Actually walking, one foot before the other, uphill, downhill?"

"What on earth would we want to do that for?" Glyn asked.

"You think of something better then."

"Why can't we do what we normally do?" said Theo.

"Let's go for a drive," said Glyn. "We'll stop at every single pub we come to and have one drink in it, and then move on. See how many pubs there are."

There are more pubs on the island than they have realised. Almost every rural community, even if it is without a shop, school, or other amenities, appears to have a pub. After the sixth pub Lara finds Theo setting off without her, in her own car. She has been to the loo and splashed her face with water, and now has to set off at a run after the two young men.

"Stop, Theo."

Under the influence of too much Black Mountain (and let us not judge the young man for his liking for that delicious Welsh apple brandy liqueur with its refreshing hint of blackcurrant, for many an older and wiser man has been seduced by the splendid elixir into drinking too much), along with the array of other drinks, like Danzy Jones and Celtic Poteen he has consumed, Theo has not realised that she is not in the car.

Fortunately he has left the passenger door open unnoticed and she is able to scramble in as he inches along at ten miles per hour. The passenger door has already acquired a scratch from scraping the stone gate post on the left. The car is too broad to pass through the gate posts with the door hanging wide open.

"Theo, let me drive," Lara insists, but he merely giggles and speeds up though she has not yet closed the door. Without a seatbelt she is in danger of falling through the open door but she manages to pull it shut. Theo is enjoying himself and he doesn't want anyone else to drive.

"For God's sake, at least take a back route," Lara tells him.

The police hang around on this road regularly, trying to catch speeding drivers. It is entirely possible that Theo does

77

not even have a licence. He doesn't own a car. He veers dangerously to the left, scraping overhanging bushes as he turns up a farm track.

The rain has been steadily increasing during this epic tour of island pubs. Too sodden on the inside with intoxicating liquor to be cognisant of what is taking place on the outside, none of the trio has noticed the tell-tale signs of a coming flood.

The floods are on the rise again in Wales. There are rocks sprouting water and new streams appearing from fissures in the rocky outcrop behind the Llewellyn-Jones's farm. The ponds and ditches fill up so that the water running down the hillside has no place to drain. Tudur and Huw begin the process of sandbagging around the doorways, and rigging up a system of pipes and troughs to channel away excess water from the farmhouse.

The water, impatient to escape the constraint of its banks, lifted its head above the grassy embankment and made a dash for the fields. It squeezed itself under and through the rails of the five bar farm gate and into the road. Not content with exiting at the gate, it also pushed itself through gaps in the stone walls either side of the gate. And Theo, driving the car along the road between two fields, found himself impeded by a foot of water which had been forced to a halt in a dip where the road was lower than anywhere else.

In the drowned fields, islands of tall spiky thistles floated here and there. The cattle gathered mournfully at the edges of the field where the ground rose slightly.

The car came to a stop as if a magic hand from the sky had arrested its progress along the road. Later the isolated cattle stranded on a shrinking island surrounded by water, in the middle of the meadow, will need rescuing by the fire brigade and volunteers in boats.

It is certain that Theo could still do most things drunk that he could do when he was sober. In fact Theo was so often drunk that his friends found it impossible to tell the difference between his drunken self and his sober self.

The sound of an approaching siren, however, renders the jovial Theo nearly frantic with the spectre of possible arrest and punishment for being drunk in control of a car. Despite the downpour he leaps from the car and flies as true as if he were an arrow fired from a bow straight through the bars of the field gate. The effects are exactly the same as if he had landed in a swimming pool and he is left struggling for breath with the icy plunge into the water. In his haste to abandon the car and its occupants, he drops the keys into the water on the other side of the gate.

It is too dark to tell whether the fleeing raft of water snatches the keys and runs away with them, or whether they merely sink. But they are not to be found. And despite earlier fervent intentions not to walk, there is no other course for the inebriated trio to take.

CHAPTER 11

THE NEW HOLYHEAD

List of contents:-
The optimism of town planners.
The benefits of reading in the loo.
How Welsh alcohol is selling well.
Theo Williams is caught pissing into a potted plant.
A preponderance of £1 shops and estate agents in Holyhead.
Ribs – but not the barbecued sort.

*

When my nephew, Dylan Jones, constructs a Lego town he begins in a dramatic fashion by heaving his enormous grey toy box, which is far too heavy for a six year old to carry, into the centre of the room, removing the lid, tipping the box until it reaches an angle at which it topples easily onto its side and spills most of its contents.

The coloured pieces of Lego then tumble higgledy piggledy onto the floor and only a discerning eye can sense the possibilities of dwellings and cars that it is theoretically possible to make from the heap of chaos lying on the bedroom carpet. My nephew is just such an idealist. Convinced he can make the city of London or the metropolis of New York rise out of the red, blue, white, yellow and grey blocks, he sets about the task as earnestly and with all the faith that a town planner might show.

The old town of Holyhead might have been constructed in the same manner that my nephew constructs his town of Lego. It sometimes appears that the hotchpotch town with buildings in varying styles, heights, shapes, all without any coherent plan that one can discern, might have been tipped out of a toy box.

The sea, used as it is to travelling between the picturesque port of Dun Laoghaire on the Irish side and Newry Beach on the Welsh side, sometimes groans when it begins its return journey to Holyhead. It lags sullenly out of reach for as long as it can, delaying its return, and then in a sudden fit of temper rushes in and hits the harbour wall, hard, as one of the ferry boats did when its pilot misjudged the sharp turn into the harbour and, instead of giving enough clearance, scraped the ship's side along the harbour wall.

Pounding the thick buttress of the stone harbour wall is all the protest that the sea can make against the gloomy misshapen skyline of Holyhead with its missed opportunities. Having viewed the pretty silhouette of Dun Laoghaire it seems an unforgiving trek back across the sea floor and once it reaches the untidy sprawling Welsh town it shuts its eyes for the night, rocking to and fro until the harbourmaster gives it the nod.

"Off you go then," the harbourmaster says. And the sea is obliged to keep its contract by ebbing to and fro in order to carry the large white ferry boats through the deep channel and out into open sea. It does it with a bad grace; petulantly flinging its arms wide, maliciously tweaking and pushing here, there, and on every side, at the vast ferry carrying the passengers. To and fro, to and fro, it rocks, sending anyone not used to its mischievous ways over to the side of the boat where a little row of heads sporting green expressions hangs over the rail. Anyone with poor sea legs foolish enough to have headed immediately for the café on embarkation will not require an explanation for why the toilets are placed immediately adjacent to the eateries on board.

As to Holyhead, there are plans afoot to transform this humble port into something that will raise it to the status of the island's jewel in the crown and make it suitable as a capital for this magic, incomparable isle. The local newspaper carried the story on its front page.

A soaring monorail is to be built above the new Holyhead, carrying passengers from the ferry port, bus stops and taxi rank, into the town in air conditioned glass pods. The shopping centre is to be enclosed in a vast crystal dome more magnificent than the Crystal Palace itself. All decrepit buildings, vandalised premises, graffiti, dirt, stray dogs, car clamps, vagrants, bag ladies, teenagers and hoodies are to be eliminated from the town centre within a short period of time, in order to raise the town to a standard of magnificence that will immediately persuade the rich shoppers, disembarking from the luxurious cruise liners anchored in the harbour, to stay in the locality and shop.

Currently there is a preponderance of second hand and charity shops, one pound and school uniform shops, plus numerous estate agents, none of which appeal to the moneyed tourists being ferried across to shore in small boats from the huge ships at anchor in the harbour. The plan is to turn Holyhead into a sort of Welsh Cannes, with all the natural beauties of sea and mountains, rivalling any Mediterranean watering hole, but without of course the climate.

These at least are Tecwyn Williams's, the architect's, ambitious plans, some of which have been adopted by those involved in the regeneration scheme, and some of which stay merely in his idealistic head and stuck to his bedroom wall with yellow post it notes.

The elevated position of his own house, above the lawyer and cockle picker's home, above the lower lying farms, above the tiny Welsh villages, has increased his appreciation of the advantages of being high up.

Like a victim of trepanning, or the bold Icarus of Greek legend, flying on wings close to the sun, the architect and his plans soar to the imaginative heights in what is appropriate for the town centre that lies within easy reach of his binoculars. The architect's own house on the hill is a wonderful spot of his own design, set above the world which he can view through his field glasses.

The myriad of corridors and passageways connecting the various sections of his own home would prove a challenge to an orienteer. It is said that you could wander around the architect's home for a whole morning together without meeting a soul, such is the labyrinthine style of the house, influenced no doubt by the Greek style which he so admires.

And certainly it is true that you could wander around the architect's house for a morning or at least for an hour, looking for someone, or rather they could wander around for an hour looking for you; as young Theo Williams did once for me. Somehow I'd got lost looking for a loo; the architect seeming to delight in siting the numerous toilets around the place in disguised locations, places you wouldn't think to look. By the time I'd spent slightly more than 60 minutes opening broom cupboards, pantries, connecting corridors hidden behind doors, I was fed up and more than desperate.

"Why are you wandering around, dancing?" Theo said, popping out of a door which apparently led somewhere. "I've been looking for you everywhere."

Once he had pointed me in the direction of one of the elusive toilets in the place, I realised why I had failed to spot it before. In fact, like Dr Who's Tardis, the loo was disguised as something else. I had looked into this room previously but had taken it to be a library because it was lined from floor to ceiling with books. I had failed to notice a small loo with the lid down in an obscure corner of the room.

Once I was seated I approved of the architect's arrangement with regard to the loo because I was fond of reading myself, and here were thousands of books just at my elbow, with a convenient seat for browsing at leisure. I didn't know whether the architect read whole books here and so developed piles from long sitting in the process, or whether he merely added to his store of knowledge in snippets, but I enjoyed examining his extensive collection.

A loo is a very useful place for keeping books because it ensures entertainment during what is inevitably a very boring ritual when performed several times a day. I personally keep two kinds of books in my loo. I keep those boring volumes in the toilet which I have been given as presents, and which I am clearly expected to read because the giver keeps asking me whether I have got to such and such a chapter yet. In order not to give offence I read these books, but very slowly, a paragraph at a time, or possibly two, depending on how long the call of nature takes and how full my bladder is, and whether my bowels need emptying or not.

The other kind of book I keep in my loo is the set I like to refer to again and again, my favourites which repay re-reading, and how better to do it than to greet them several times a day, depending on the frequency of my trips and how many cups of tea I have drunk?

Thus I keep in my loo copies of *Horrible Histories* (good for a laugh if having a quick pee, a Bible (a gift – and the reason I am never short of a Bible quotation or two). It can be a bit hard going in parts, like the genealogies and old battles, but there are a few enlivening bits, like the appearance of a naked Bathsheba bathing on her roof and David, like the architect regularly peering from his roof across the landscape viewing the locality and the antics of his neighbours, clapping eyes on her juicy flesh. A bit salacious but as good as a soap. My Bible, like the copy of Chaucer's *Canterbury Tales* which always falls open at the Miller's Tale, always seems to fall open at the racy bits.

There's a complete set of Jane Austen on my loo window (good when constipated), *The Complete Wholefood Recipe Guide* (seems like a good idea when constipated), the *Mabinogion* (because I didn't quite finish it in school), John Mortimer's *Famous Trials* (exciting when you're stuck),

84

miscellaneous volumes of poetry (short for when you're in a hurry) and one or two others which I shan't bother to list. Having only a small bathroom, Martyn and I are hampered for space. The architect was able to indulge himself by housing a loo in his library, rather than putting a few books in the loo.

It was fortunate that Theo appeared when he did because I was so desperate for relief from the burden of carrying a full bladder, that I was eyeing the potted palm with its large decorated bowl containing earth, on one of the upper storeys, which looked as though it needed a bit of watering. Fortunately the potted palm proved to be unnecessary for which I was glad. Only utter desperation would have driven me to the extremity of weeing on someone's house plant ever since I had been warned, by Theo's own tale, of the dangers attached to such an action.

Theo has the seemingly unenviable occupation of acting as sales representative for a company selling home-produced Welsh alcoholic drinks. A poorly paid job you might think? Not a bit of it. If he had been able to drive (he had already failed four driving tests due to his failure to look in the mirrors), Theo would easily have been able to buy a decent car. Welsh alcohol is on the up and doing very well thank you.

On one of his trips around the country, Theo had taken to sampling his own company's products with which, I hasten to say, they kept him well-supplied, thus he had no need to drink any of the profits, or slip a bit on the side as they say. Being a generous soul, he had shared his tipple with a group of drinking pals – he had a drinking set in all the locations he was required to sell in – in a restaurant that was not licensed but which welcomed patrons with their own drinks.

On returning to his hotel at night, thoroughly sloshed, he found he'd forgotten his room key and was utterly desperate for the loo into the bargain. His brain befogged by the fumes of alcohol, he omitted to call reception for another key, and pissed instead into the potted plant standing on the floor of the corridor.

It was unfortunate that the hotel's CCTV camera was trained on that very potted plant, and even more unfortunate that it developed a glitch that very night exactly at the spot on the tape which recorded Theo pissing vigorously into the plant pot, and even missing the pot a little due to the urgency of nature's call. Consequently the tape got stuck at Theo's crucial moment and kept replaying the scene over and over again to the bemusement of the security guard called to view it.

As a valued client the hotel management were not inclined to quarrel with Theo over a potted plant, but sheer embarrassment led Theo to choose another, less favoured, hotel in the town for, as he said, he hated having to pass the security guard who also doubled as a door attendant at slack periods.

It is not beyond the scope of the architect's ambitions to envisage a space port in the environs of the town which at present only houses a ferry port. An occasional sight of the Aurora Borealis from the summit of his hill has encouraged him frequently to look skywards. Indeed, whether the architect looks upwards or downwards there are many remarkable things within his sphere of vision.

Just one season at his window with the binoculars – and it is acknowledged truly that no house within a 3 mile radius of the Lobster Pot is without a pair of binoculars – has produced a veritable pageant of extraordinary activity: An oil rig making a journey at the end of a tow rope destined for Scotland; several air and sea rescues by the RAF (and only one rescue botched) with airmen dangling from helicopters on ropes attempting to rescue persons from the sea who have been planted there for the purpose of rescuing. To my knowledge their record of achievement is excellent with only one attempt producing injury to the participants rather than effecting a rescue.

There is another activity which the enthusiastic observer termed, "The ribs" which for a while puzzled me. The architect so regularly and often referred to these ribs, that I was embarrassed to admit my ignorance about them. Initially I assumed we were talking about spare ribs of the barbecued variety but when the architect kept referring to them as having been, "Out at sea and vast in size," it became clear that whatever they were, they were not coated with a sauce as they are at the Chinese takeaway.

I had hidden my ignorance about the ribs for so long that it became absolutely impossible to admit to the architect that, in fact, I knew nothing whatsoever about them. Fortunately it emerged in a chance conversation I had with a neighbour that the solution to the mystery of the ribs was to be found in a Holyhead boatyard where they were building them.

Having thus unravelled the mystery and deduced that they were the ribs or skeletons of boats, I agreed to accompany the architect on a visit to the boatyard where the boat builders seemed rather bemused at receiving visitors as though they were somehow a tourist attraction, and they apologetically told the architect that they did not speak to unexpected visitors who had no appointment between the hours of 9-1 or 2-5 due to the heavy workload they were labouring under but that he would be very welcome to come and chat in the lunch hour.

CHAPTER 12

PROBLEM SOLVING

List of contents:-

*

The Catholic priest was hot and restless in bed. The cantankerous pheasant outside his window shouted "2 am."

"Bloody pheasant," the priest intoned, and then crossed himself to make amends.

"Exorcism," he muttered, going back to the paper on pastoral care with which he was enlivening the night in the absence of sleep. *Demonic possession of individuals and the necessity of exorcism should be carefully distinguished from cases where individuals merely have psychiatric problems* he read.

The priest turned, shifted onto his left side, stiff from lying so long on his right side.

"3 am," the brightly coloured pheasant squawked fiercely. The bird was lacking a mate. With its fine gold and brown back, black beady eyes rimmed with red feathers, he was an attractive enough bird to have summoned a harem of pale brown females if he chose.

The hedgehog snorted derisively as it trotted across the presbytery garden, sniffing here and there for a bowlful of bread and milk. He found a cracked brown bowl in a corner by the wall with dried-on cat food. The priest's generosity usually extended itself to the hedgehogs, but the thieving presbytery cat had been by earlier.

"4 am," the pheasant intoned sonorously.

At 5 am the priest's slippers groaned as he shuffled his cold feet into them. The creaking floorboard close to the bed lifted its head curiously at the approach of footsteps but lay back down again with a sigh.

"Go to sleep," the floorboards whisper. "Go to sleep." But the pacing up and down continues.

The wind continues its knocking at the doors and windows. It looks down the chimney and gives long low whistles. The mist shrugs its shoulders uneasily, wriggling its way over fields, ditches and gullies, slipping round the corner at Steffan Bach's farmhouse but stopping short at the next farm.

Although it was still dark and his favourite Radio 4 programmes had not yet begun, the priest decided to have breakfast.

I always think that one of the most difficult problems is working out an approach to life. If, like Fr Tristan, one cannot attempt any task without working out how to do it first, then life becomes full of unresolved problems, unfinished tasks, uncertainties, questions, and possibly lack of success.

Take the other day for instance. Breakfast was the first hurdle. Whether to eat frosted flakes, or brown bread and butter with honey, or muesli, or coffee and croissant was the first issue of the day.

89

Fr Tristan often woke up feeling that he was at the top of a tall slide, hesitating about taking the ride down, needing a big push to set him on the way of another big day in life.

Should he go for the sweet option, sugared flakes of corn at the start of a day burdened with decisions? There was always the healthy option if he felt like prolonging his anxious existence for a few years longer. He could adopt a routine if he wanted to take the easy way out. No more decisions, he thought. He would take coffee and croissant every day. Yet the coffee and croissant option seemed to pose such philosophical problems that he was forced to reconsider the matter.

If he adopted a routine was he merely swapping the uncertainties of existence for unthinking security? His moral character and ability to make decisions could certainly be affected by taking the coffee and croissant route, he reflected. Not to mention his taste buds which would rise in resistance at an unvarying diet of white bread each morning. Well of course he could do them in rotation but then that's the easy way out isn't it? It's routine again but just another routine. One would certainly have to debate the advantages of one routine over another.

No. Let's settle this question once and for all, he decided. Instead of coffee and croissant every day, he would have cornflakes on Monday, bread and honey on Tuesday, muesli on Wednesday and croissant on Thursday.

By this time he was sorely in need of breakfast to remove the dilemma and the headache that had set in even before breakfast had begun. He chose something on the weak grounds of a hungry stomach and the fact that dawn was breaking.

He discovered however that the muesli packet was virtually empty and destitute of the best bit of cereal anyway. There were no whole almonds left. That settled it. Bread and honey it was.

But the thing he detested most of all had occurred and left him fretting and fuming in such an ill humour that he would shortly need an aspirin to relieve him of the headache and despondent mood that had settled on him.

Whoever had been at the honey before him had plunged the knife with which they were buttering their bread into the jar and left traces of crumbs and butter in the smooth yellow honey. Tristan was furious. This had obviously happened several times since he last tasted the honey because there was a slight grey fluff growing in the jar. The nausea that turned his stomach when he pictured spreading butter, honey and mould on his bread caused a major upset even before the day had fairly begun.

The sugared flakes seemed to be his only option but he was afflicted by notions that he would become one of those unhealthy obese citizens whose size and dietary habits are constantly discussed in the newspapers.

Dawn had definitely broken by now and the priest's stomach was rumbling with hunger. Breakfast had not yet begun and how, he wondered, was he to find time for all the other decisions of the day? Particularly the one about what he was going to wear to the grand St Tudno hotel in Llandudno where a dinner given in honour of one of his congregation, a professor at the university, was going to be held.

This distinguished professor, who had taught Father Tristan when he was at the university, was the same one who regularly appears on television as an expert in his subject. There are one or two wicked rumours going around that he spends so much time on his appearance and on presenting that he no longer has time for his subject or for producing any new research, but we do not listen to such unkind whispers.

There is a reprehensible side to the professor's character, however, known only to one or two people. The man with a string of letters after his name grew up in the city of Manchester, close to the university museum, where he spent his Saturdays wandering around the butterfly collection and the stuffed animals. Being a city boy he had never seen alive the specimens of lepidopterists and taxidermists. His enthusiasm for the art of stuffing and his appreciation of a well-constructed glass eye, the poised wing of a dead eagle, or a beautifully preserved Adonis Blue fastened by a pin, has stayed with him into adulthood and seeped into his soul.

There is a drawer in a dark, inaccessible corner of the professor's home study where a few beautiful blue specimens of butterfly lie speared with pins; there is the odd ivory ornament, an elephant's foot holder for pencils, a snakeskin bag and one or two other unidentifiable objects made of hide or skin.

It is a moral for those who are not taught religion at a young age; there is always something else to take its place, and in the professor's case it is a worship of all things natural. Unlike the Celts, moved to adore the spirits of water and land, however, the professor is not interested in spirits, merely in the inanimate beauty of skewered moths and detached limbs. It is also a sad tale of our cities where mushrooms are picked from boxes and apples from shelves. It is hardly the professor's fault that he admires his elephant's foot pencil holder, detached from the leg of the elephant, when he had only ever seen plums or apples severed from the limbs of trees before he was age eighteen.

Like his more famous colleague Professor Vladimir Nabokov, that literary superstar and author of *Lolita*, whose alternative profession was that of lepidopterist, the professor is a lover of blue butterflies.

Who knows whether the decline in the species of Silver Studded Blue, a rare butterfly of North Wales, might not be due to the professor's skill with his net? And if there are one or two fewer of the rare Adonis Blue in its southern habitat, it may be connected with the fact that the professor takes his holidays down south where the climate is warmer than here in North Wales.

The Common Blue butterfly may not be as common as it once was thanks to the professor's activities, and the Small Blue, although not decreasing in size, may be living up to its name in terms of population numbers if the professor has a say in the matter.

The difference between the professor from Manchester and his Russian colleague is that the lepidoptery habits of the first are secret and illegal, unlike the man of letters who thought and dreamed of a career dedicated to the study and preservation of butterflies and when he was not writing stories about sexual slavery, wrote tomes about fabulous blue butterflies.

This professor was also the same one who would drop his papers onto the floor and run from the lectern on the dais to the window to watch the Anglesey RAF jets fly over the university at high speed. He looked up at the skies above the university with his curiously colourless eyes, tinged with only a slight grey tone, due to having spent most of his early years looking down and examining city streets, grey pavements and roads.

"Vroom," the professor said, as the down draught from the planes nearly ripped the roof of the lecture hall from above his head.

The priest does not share the professor's enthusiasm for the jets. He hears the faint ghostlike, "Ach ach ach," sound of guns, and pictures prostrate bodies with no breath or life left in them when he sees the war machines cross the sky. He was once in the local newspaper for joining the protestors lying down on the airfield, trying to prevent the jets taking to the air during an unpopular war.

Father Tristan's aversion to jets has made him unpopular with his bishop who collects model aeroplanes. The bishop has model World War II aeroplanes, made from kits, hanging from his bedroom ceiling. He lies on his back admiring them before he switches off the bedside light at night.

The St Tudno hotel was a surprise to the priest. With its dinky wrought iron bench suitable only for two thin people to sit side by side, its symmetrical marble tiles, carefully cut miniature evergreen bushes distributed evenly on either side of the shiny white path leading to a dense and glossy green arch which would be a grand size for elves, it looked smaller, more reassuring then some of the bigger hotels at the other end of the promenade.

During the evening Father Tristan watched the spectacle of a tall grey haired man approach a nearby table with the manner of someone greeting old friends. This was the proprietor himself. Fr Tristan sat silently, twiddling with his third inner fork, feeling like he had at inspection time when he had been a member of the Sea Cadets in his youth. Tristan had an excellent memory and a few revolutions brought it back to the occasions on which his uniform had failed to pass muster with the authorities.

As the proprietor approached Tristan's table, the priest lowered his blue eyes to the tablecloth, and twiddled his dog collar and cuff links in alarm, wondering whether his attire was going to pass muster. He felt the same relief this time, when the proprietor beamed at him and offered a welcome, as he did on the occasions when the dentist told him that he did not require any fillings in his teeth.

Fr Tristan was a little nervous that night on leaving the hotel. He saw a few youths with hoods in that town built along the shore with its long arm sticking out into the sea. There were misshapen letters of black spray paint on the walls of one of the shops. He noticed some hopeless scrawl at the rail station and writing in black sloping lines on a bus shelter. Like King Nebuchadnezzar he tried to decipher the writing on the wall. He hardly knew what it was that frightened him but it was something he saw as he looked out of the window of the hotel.

The priest looked out of the window at the dark. The sea was rising and falling like water in a bowl being tipped from side to side. It was the place where the lights stopped and ran into the impenetrable blackness of the sea on a night with no stars. Fr Tristan sensed the invisible coils of rope that sometimes gripped his arms beginning to knot him to the chair. His fingers and toes tightened under the table. He noticed with alarm that his watch had speeded up and that time was wasting at three times its normal rate and that it was getting very late. He looked out of the window and saw a lamp post flicker and go out.

In a reversal of the creation scriptures, one moment there was light, and the next a shadow in the night. He kept trying to breathe.

"In. Out," he told himself. "In. Out."

"Are you alright, Father?" his neighbour at the table enquired.

Father Tristan picked up his glass. The water leapt out of the glass of its own volition and tipped itself down his shirt front. The priest looked for the napkin on his knee, only to find that it had remained folded on the table during the meal.

After leaving the mainland, crossing the bridge to Anglesey, and speeding back over the isle at midnight, Father Tristan saw the ghost of Ireland on the water when the sea was lit by the moon. He knew that this was a good omen and he showed his white teeth in the mirror as he drove home.

The following day, however, the omen seemed to belie its significance when he realised that it was the day for confessions. The hour for confessions usually found Fr Tristan blowing into a paper bag outside the confessional box.

"Must I really go in?" he gasped to Sister Glenys, the nun delegated by the bishop to help soothe the priest on these anxious occasions. "Do I really have to go in there?

You never know what you might hear in there. Do I really have to?"

The last question uttered tremulously to his shoes invites the Sister's hand on his arm and her soothing, "There, there, Father. I really think you should. I'm just out here if you need me. It'll be alright I'm sure. Probably nothing you haven't heard before."

The priest looked with hope at the line of penitents sitting queuing on the pew by the wall. Then he looked out of the church window at the telephone wire where dozens of starlings were swinging like clothes pegs on a washing line. At the sudden movement of the presbytery cat, the starlings rose shrieking into the air and flew away. Father Tristan sighed and went into the confessional box.

In the evening he was puzzled again by the seeming failure of his omen in seeing Ireland's ghost upon the water on the western side of Anglesey. He peered down into the tea leaves at the bottom of his mug as if seeking confirmation, like a priest peering over the entrails looking for a positive augury.

The curtains gave a shiver in the draught from the window and the telephone waked from sleep, giving several loud trills. Like the trials of Job, or funerals which always come in bunches of three, tribulations tended to come in multiples and today was no exception as the priest heard the voice of his superior, the bishop, skittering down the phone wire.

The bishop was exceedingly cautious about relations with churches of other denominations. He was afraid that if he allowed grace to seep out of the church and into other channels, that the conduits of grace may cease to function. To avoid wasting grace or seeing it spread too thinly by being allowed to escape from its usual sacramental channels of Mass, penance and confession and into less worthy channels, he imposed a rigid paternal discipline on the priests who answered to him.

Like the good servant taking care of his master's coins, he was parsimonious in allowing the divine favour to flow from the purse and took good care that the coins of grace should be given only to worthy recipients, the good folk of his own flock, and not those outside the church or in other communions, lest the sacred channels of grace should run dry.

The bishop enjoyed telling his favourite joke every year at the priests' conference. Whether he noticed that there were no new priests and he was telling the same joke to the same priests who had heard it for ten years running, I cannot say. He reminded Fr Tristan of it now.

"Father, do you remember the Welshman who was shipwrecked alone on a desert island?"

Father Tristan did remember.

"He built two chapels on that island. Why was that now? Can you guess why he built the second chapel?"

"The second one was the one he didn't go to," repeated Father Tristan automatically.

The bishop hooted with laughter down the phone.

"That's right," he said. "The second chapel was the one he didn't go to. Always remember that my boy. There's always a right place and a wrong place, and a right way and a wrong way to do things. Remember that."

This joke always gave Tristan a headache because he had puzzled for ten years over his inability to explain the punch line. He continually felt that he lacked the bishop's intellect.

"I'm going to tell that one at the priests' conference next month," the bishop confided.

There was a tremor which began somewhere around the level of the priest's neck, tapped its way down the bones of his spinal column and found its way down through his knees into his feet. There was a chair beside the telephone. The priest sat on it and examined the scuff marks made by the scores of boys who had sat on this chair and kicked their feet whilst waiting to be examined on the catechism.

"The good servant uses his master's coins wisely," the bishop's manner of delivery rarely changed whether he was addressing the cathedral congregation or one solitary priest on the other end of the phone.

The priest, it seemed, had been spending the coins unwisely by doling them out right, left and centre to lapsed Catholics, divorced and remarried parishioners, Anglicans, and those of other dubious persuasions. The priest, "Must not throw pearls before swine," the bishop admonished.

As the downcast Father Tristan stared at the floor he saw a small black beetle scrambling hurriedly over the wooden floorboards. It met the obstacle of a table leg at which it pushed frantically for some minutes, trying to climb vertically up the wooden post before toppling finally onto its back with its black spiky legs floundering helplessly in the air. The priest helped the small beetle back onto its feet by gently flipping it over with the edge of his toe.

The bishop's slightly high pitched tones had begun to merge with the whittering of the starlings which settled into the tree in the garden whenever the presbytery cat failed to do its duty. Never was a collective noun more correctly applied than a *murmuration* of starlings to those chattering, self-important little creatures.

Whenever he was specially agitated or nervous the hapless priest found himself uttering nonsense words under his breath.

"Kerplop!" he said. And "Ker-ching"! Or sometimes, "Katang," or "Knickers!"

"I beg your pardon?" asked the bishop.

Sometimes Father Tristan was so engrossed in his embarrassment that he hardly noticed whether he were saying the nonsensical words aloud or not. The same problem had sometimes occurred when he was talking to his parishioners. Occasionally he made an embarrassing slip in a

98

sermon and felt compelled to apologise for it. But the apology, albeit under his breath, generally came out as, "Kerplop!" Or several kerplops if he was very unlucky. How to explain the kerplops both to himself and to others was a problem that left his cheeks mottled with an infusion of beetroot red colour.

He had said, "Kerplop" to the bishop a month earlier when his Lordship had arrived unexpectedly early for a working lunch. Tristan had been vacuuming the dining room carpet, in anticipation of an inspection of his regimen by his superior in the religious hierarchy, when a fat queen bee apparently resting on the carpet had been sucked into the machine. Conscience-stricken by the idea of a hive minus its queen, he quickly pulled the plug and opened up the vacuum cleaner. A cloud of dust had flown out. Fearful of the bishop's eagle eye for dust, the priest carried the machine into the garden.

Carefully sorting through the dust on the grass, he found the queen, smothered in hairs and carpet fluff but still alive. He ran indoors for his thin paint brush which he sometimes used for landscapes and water-colours and carefully brushed the bee free of dust. Absorbed in cleaning, he did not hear the bishop's car, a nasty sound of scraping paintwork as the bishop manoeuvred his large car awkwardly through the gate posts, catching his wing as he did so, and the curse that followed.

The first he heard of the bishop was, "What are you grovelling on the floor like a dog for, Tristan?"

"I'm brushing this bee," the priest volunteered timidly. And then, involuntarily, "Kerplop," by way of apology for not having met the bishop at the door.

The bishop rolled his eyes. "Get me a cup of tea," he said wearily. "Your gate post has scratched my car."

Father Tristan reached into his pocket for a handkerchief as he sat listening to the bishop on the phone. He pulled out a square piece of paper, a lottery ticket which

Sister Glenys usually bought for him during the week. He amused himself in spare moments when he had nothing to do by shaking his lottery pen, which he used to help him choose numbers for the weekly lottery, and watching the balls with numbers on tumble out from the round container on the top of the pen, down into a thin straight line. He had a newspaper. There was time to check the numbers against the ticket while the bishop's words found their way through his digestive system and out the other end.

CHAPTER 13

THE BARD'S SONG

List of contents:-
A trip to hear the Welsh bard.
The bard bakes his stories in the oven.
The bard's house catches fire and burns to the ground.
Rhiannon's magic birds.
Owain Glyndŵr – hero of the Welsh nation.

*

Tudur's birthday present to his sister Gwyneth was an outing to hear the Welsh bard.

The storyteller's stories came straight out of the oven, a big wood burning stove in his hut, that baked hot fresh Welsh bread on two days of the week and baked stories on all the other days.

A few minutes after the stories came hot out of the oven, the storyteller turned the tins upside down, gave a sharp tap on the base, and out they came, done to a turn with the steam still rising. He laid the stories out on a metal rack to cool before examining them. He served the stories to his guests along with tea and Welsh cakes.

On summer evenings when his audience came from the length and breadth of Wales, the stars lent their beams as spotlights and the trees hunched their green capes together to form a canopy and leaned down towards the bard. His audience sat in a circle around a fire and listened to the tales from the *Mabinogion* or to the heroic tales about Owain Glyndŵr.

The bard threw his logs on the fire and the perfume of pine and birch wood crept its way into the nostrils of the audience. Gwyneth Llewellyn-Jones unfastened her sandals and then fastened them again in expectation. The owl restrained its hoot and leaned forwards intently on the branch in order to hear.

The power of the bard's stories are legendary in these parts. Often he has set fire to the vegetation, the greenery spontaneously bursting into flame, with excitement at the tales of Celtic heroism. On one such occasion the storyteller's round house too caught light and burnt to a cinder long before the fire brigade was able to arrive.

The flames of the fire were fanned by the potent story of the magic birds of Rhiannon, a death goddess and the bringer of dreams, who could sing so sweetly, like the Sirens of old, that men were lured to their deaths. These birds sang from the underworld for the companions of Bran, an old King of this mighty isle, when his remains were carried by his comrades from Wales to London. The singing of these birds took place at Harlech and the beauty of their voices held the men enraptured for seven years in that place.

The bard conjured Rhiannon's birds for the benefit of his hushed audiences until it was believed that the birds could be heard singing from under the earth. The fire leapt out of its restraints and licked the walls of the storyteller's hut in a burning frenzy of longing for the magical siren singer. Even the powerful hoses of three combined fire brigades found it hard to cool the ardour of the fire which burned until morning.

On this occasion, with Tudur and Gwyneth in the audience, the notes of the bard's voice ascended into the air in crotchets and quavers until a full orchestra was playing in the ether.

"Friends and fellow Welshmen," the bard sang, "The story of our greatest fellow countryman, Owain Glyndŵr, who was descended from the princes of Powys and, as even the great English poet Shakespeare says, *he was not in the roll of common men*. His home was at Sycharth with its grey slate roof, its green park, fish pond and mill: A home to deer roaming on the hoof; a heronry of birds with long flowing tail feathers; the fertile soil, the emerald grass and the daffodil."

Owain Glyndŵr, like all the warrior heroes of old, employed his own bard, Iolo Goch, to sing his praises and to tell the stories of Welsh valour against the English in battle. The villainous King Henry IV outlawed the noble storytellers and bards, but their stories and tales of heroic deeds escaped into the Welsh villages and mountains with the outlaws. The birds hid the tales in their feathers, insects carried them on their wings, and the winds dispersed the stories to every corner of the Welsh nation.

The story-maker warmed to his theme of the Welsh nobleman and his revolt against the English oppressor; and then his final retreat to the hills with a small band of men.

When the bard reached the part of the story where Owain Glyndŵr was laid to rest, like King Arthur of the Round Table, in a cave sealed with magic enchantments, awaiting his second coming; sleeping in a secret mountain dell, with his horse at hand, saddled, ready to wake and engage in battle with the perfidious English nation again, Gwyneth Llewellyn-Jones shivered with delight.

Even the snake in the bushes, which had been about to seize a fledgling, stilled the flickering of its forked tongue, and let the bird go. A snail paused silently in its slippery track. The frog swallowed its croak and the grass kept a reverent hush. The storyteller breathed red fire into the air and the last smoke rings ascended towards the trees. A few tears dripped from a cloud but evaporated in the heat from the fire.

"When is Owain Glyndŵr going to come again and fight the English?" Gwyneth whispered to Tudur in the shadows leaping from the orange fire. An echo caught her voice, sent its notes high into the air and threw them back again into the centre of the story telling circle.

The Welsh bard tugged his beard and continued narrating.

"The Welsh students at Oxford sold their books and travelled home to fight at Owain Glyndŵr's side, and the labourers in the fields of Shropshire and Herefordshire downed their tools to come to the aid of the red dragon. The blood of many of our finest sons, the flower of the Welsh nobility was spilt in the cause of our nation against the English aggressor."

There are few men in this world who bear as many of the hallmarks of true heroism as Owain Glyndŵr. Like the indomitable Homeric warriors of old he engaged in ten years of warfare against the enemy; before escaping like the Icenic Queen Boudicaa before him to the wilds with a small band of outlaws in order to escape the perfidy of the enemy. And like the famed King Arthur of the Round Table, he sleeps, in an unmarked place, awaiting his second coming.

In the morning when Gwyneth accompanied her mother in dropping Rhodri and Alun at their school, two words of graffiti emblazoned in black across the wall of the school caught her eyes. *Meibion Glyndŵr*. She tugged her mother's arm.

"Look. It says Glyndŵr over there. Does it mean Glyndŵr has come back now, Mam?"

"Those are the Sons of Glyndŵr," Anni told her. "They burn down the houses of English people in Wales."

Gwyneth shivered delightedly. "Just like Glyndŵr," she said.

Anni sighed. There was the butter, cheese, yoghurt and clotted cream still to make, the bread to prove for a second time, the jam to label, and the cakes to bake. One of her jam-making English friends at the Women's Institute had been visited in the dark by Meibion Glyndŵr, who were leaving their painted black signature on many a fine blank wall and post box, and she was now afraid to sleep in her bed at night. The rustle of leaves in the wind made her start up and look out of her bedroom window, expecting to see crackling flames licking their way up her walls.

Anni wondered whether she should begin a list of occasions on which rape and pillage had received the approval of storytellers and bards, and become part of glorious folk history, and when it was merely rape and pillage. Like other notions the question faded away under the pressure of cheese, bread and yoghurt-making. And under the pressure of another arrival.

Just as the goddess Athene leapt fully armed from the head of her father Zeus, Eiluned's baby leapt out of womb on the stroke of midnight with his fists curled in the posture of a boxer.

"Can we call him Owain. Please. Pleeeease," said Gwyneth. And Owain Llewellyn-Jones he was.

It goes without saying that the latest addition to the Llewellyn-Jones family was a prodigy, and to prove it I can relate that the infant had two front teeth from birth and weighed in at a full twelve pounds.

CHAPTER 14

GHOSTS AND RED SQUIRRELS

List of contents:-
The grey intruders and the necessity of deportation.
How the squirrels got here – probably across the bridge since they are unlikely to swim.
No leprechauns on the housing list.
A ghost does the fandango.
Ghosts come with the furniture.
Idris Davies's cold wife.
Fetching the spoon in an unorthodox way and how Idris Davies found his wife out.

*

Anglesey is one of the few refuges in this country for our native species of red squirrel. For those persons of a certain age who were taken in their pushchairs by their mothers to become bona fide members of the Tufty Club in those old pre-school days, the image of a red squirrel carries with it a certain nostalgia and a memory of orange squash and custard creams before one's mother came to take one home again for lunch.

Although I must admit, despite having attended the Tufty Club myself at age 3, that I have not always been as fond of squirrels as this image implies, having once lived in a house adjacent to a copse riddled with squirrels who regularly made their way in at my bathroom window, knocking over my bath salts, or stole into the pantry and unscrewed the jars of Nutella.

I am very fond of a slice of toast in the mornings spread with Nutella and to find the jar had been raided yet again by a pair of thieving grey hands was enough to drive away my appetite. Given that the grey furry intruder was little more than some kind of a rat, I was perturbed to find its tiny hand prints inside the nut and chocolate spread and along the tiled floor of the pantry.

How it is that grey squirrels began to make inroads to this isle, this sanctuary and haven for red squirrels, is unknown, but the little blighters have got here somehow. The powers-that-be have decided to take the only upright course open to right-thinking patriots and deport the unwelcome asylum seekers immediately. If all government departments were as efficient in rounding up and transporting without protest or appeal such vast numbers of unwanted visitors, they would rightly receive praise and accolades for their efficiency. Alas, such efficiency does not exist in every field of public life.

To my certain knowledge at least a couple of thousand of the grey intruders have been rounded up and deported elsewhere. Although I am unsure of the exact location of their exile, I can only assert the moral improbability, the sheer unlikelihood, the total impossibility in fact, of a perfidious suggestion that has been wafting about on the tail feathers of a rumour bird or two.

It has been whispered that a few of the unwelcome denizens have found their way to London where a certain cooked delicacy has made it into the repertoire of chefs in the capital. However, my own faith in the falsity of these rumours is total and I pass on, merely adding that although I deplore the invasion of these foreigners with bland grey coats, and patriotically uphold the native rights and privileges of the red fur brigade, I would by no means wish to see the foreigners mistreated or kept otherwise than in humane conditions.

It is my conviction that the furry illegal immigrants have been deported to some distant wooded colony to live out their days stripping the trees of bark and denuding the birds' nests of their eggs, and all the other heinous offences of which they are suspected.

How the infiltrators and illegal immigrants got onto this fair isle in the first place is a question of some interest. Experts have asserted that they must either have swum over from the mainland, or crossed one of the two bridges linking Anglesey to the mainland of Wales, since there is no other route.

Despite offering a reward for proof of a scientific nature that the grey squirrels, being of obviously lower intelligence than the red variety, can swim, I have as yet received no news or photographs on the subject of squirrels doing the breaststroke, or any other kind of stroke for that matter. Nor has anyone enlightened me as to what the squirrels may possibly do with their tails when they swim, seeing that swimming squirrels would be burdened by nothing less than a big bushy brush on their backsides as they swim which would grow wetter and heavier as they swam on further.

No it is clear to me that the squirrels have crossed either the Britannia Bridge or the Menai Suspension Bridge in their quest for a home. It is even possible that they may have made the journey by train which runs across the Britannia Bridge to Holyhead, or even possibly by boat.

In addition to squirrels there have been a few unpatriotic assertions from across the sea by our Hibernian neighbour that one or two of its small green denizens have removed themselves from its jurisdiction, and that the likeliest place of their arrival is on our shores. But I dismiss this at once. Wherever Ireland's leprechauns have decamped to it is not likely, I think, that they would come here. And it is a fact, for it has been checked with the relevant official departments, that no one very small, or green, or answering to the description of a leprechaun has either registered for council housing or enlisted at the institutions and courses for learning the Welsh language.

However, onto the matter which concerns me now, which is the likelihood that Wales is one of the most haunted places in the entire world.

If, like me, you are one of life's more gullible characters, a real sucker for *true* stories, then the words, "And it really happened," will instantly engage one's credulity and belief in the particular ghost whose specific style of haunting is the subject of the story, and induce goose bumps up the arms. However it is not necessary for me to expound on the likelihood of my being taken in by such stories when there are much greater experts in the matter whose faith in these matters cannot be impugned.

Morgan Davies's octogenarian father has long been visited by his own irascible dead father on long winter evenings. When he was alive the old man, Dewi Davies by name, used to sit tapping his fingers impatiently by candlelight in the armchair by the fire and, according to the Davies's, he still sits there of an evening, or at least his fingers do, tapping a fandango for all they are worth.

Given that Morgan Davies's eighty year old father, Arwel, is also drawn to tapping his fingers in the same way, there are as many as twenty fingers tapping fandangos on the chair arms of an evening. It is doubtful that either Dewi or Arwel, both Welsh speakers and taciturn into the bargain, had ever heard the word *fandango* but, nevertheless, it is an apt description for their lively style of dancing with fingers.

Old Dewi Davies always went to bed at the same time each night and so ingrained had the farmer's habits become that he still carried them on even after death. His footsteps could be heard at the same hour of night, crossing the landing and banging the door to his room, which is now Morgan's room. But Morgan is so used to the sound of creaking floorboards and the door slamming that he never turns a hair.

He does not bother with cleaning his teeth in the evenings nor with changing his underpants more than twice a week, but there is hope for the old sinner yet because he kneels beside his bed at night to pray for, "Good luck, and a good crop of potatoes," before getting under the covers, and waiting for his bedroom door to bang before turning on his side to sleep. If the bed dips slightly at one side and if there is a vague tapping of fingers on the bedside table, Morgan is off to sleep so quickly that he does not notice. The Davies's are used to sharing beds with chilly partners and it was most probably part of his dream anyway. In fact, so familiar is he with the spirit's routine that a cessation in it would produce an eerie silence indeed.

It is an odd thing that a person should be so attached to the routines performed by his hands and feet that these are the only things that remain of him. But so it is that the hands refuse to part company with the chair and the feet refuse to desist from their nightly walk along the corridor. It is a strange thing that here in our Celtic country we are fascinated by spirits and ghosts and that they are actively sought out by ghost hunters. Unlike the Welsh, Thai people, for instance, are terrified by ghosts and do not wish to own antiques or possessions which have belonged to a deceased person in case the previous owner's ghost comes attached to the item of furniture.

The Davies family has had a long association with ghosts and spirits of the nether world. During the Napoleonic Wars an ancestor of Morgan Davies married a lady of Aberffraw, a place long associated with problems of the heart. They had barely been married a few months when the unfortunate man was sent off to fight the infamous Frenchman. Luckily, having survived Waterloo, Morgan's ancestor was able to return to his wife and new-born child in Wales and his family life resumed where it had left off.

The only difference in his home that Idris Davies could detect was a drop in the temperature. No matter how many logs he put on the fire, he could never restore the house to its former warmth. The man chopped and chopped at logs, felling virtually every tree in the place to warm up his home, but to no avail. He shivered in his bed at night, two blocks of ice replacing his feet in the dark hours. His wife was equally icy and the poor man could not warm himself against her because any squeeze of her waist or caress chilled him to the bone.

Life went on in this deep freeze of a house for two months until one night when Idris Davies was sitting at the table over a good hot thick broth, hoping to warm his belly and limbs with the steaming liquid. He shouted at his wife to bring him a spoon since the lady had forgotten to put spoons on the table. Instead of getting up from the table, the woman reached out her arm and put it through the wall into the kitchen and fetched the spoon that way. And that was how Idris Davies knew he had been living with a ghost for two months.

The poor bride had died after giving birth to the baby but her devotion to her new husband being so great, she had decided to wait around for him anyway to return from the war. She was very reluctant to leave her home even after the spoon incident and Idris Davies was driven to desperation they say in his attempts to drive his ghostly wife from his house.

Truly it is said that a man's devotion is never of the same quality as a woman's. Having refused to allow death to step in the way of her reunion with her husband, the woman's faithfulness was not repaid by an equal loyalty. After filling the house with prickly scrub and sharp butchering knives to deter her from entering, just as scoundrels try to keep fairy folk out of their homes when they have lost the favour of those spirits, he had to resort to calling a priest and performing an exorcism since the lady

111

was determined not to leave him, even if he had decided to divorce her.

Idris Davies's house was finally exorcised of his wife's spirit but not of the chill that had taken hold since the woman's death. He was forced to live with the cold until his own death many years later. It is an unfortunate thing for the Davies family that they are always cold in their extremities but it seems to be a gene thing and no cure for it.

CHAPTER 15

HOLIDAY HOMES

List of contents:-
The unlucky nature of holiday homes and a warning to avoid them.
A case of mushroom poisoning.

*

Holiday homes are an unlucky subject on this otherwise lucky isle. To take a case in point, the small traditional cottage named Glyndŵr, after our great Welsh hero, has seen off many an unwary owner. Like many a holiday home or cottage kept for rent it was gradually deteriorating in the strong sea winds which delight in taking the paint and artex from the walls, pulling at the guttering, and cuffing the TV aerial so that it sits lopsided on the roof.

A mouse or two had moved in with every intention of remaining, and from the septic tank situated not far from the kitchen window arose such a stink that on a hot summer's day it rivalled Stinking Bishop cheese for pungency. Various builders and property repairers had come and gone. Gone being the operative word. It was impossible for the owner to exercise authority over and take a superior tone with someone who had turned up his nose at the smell of his septic tank. The distant English owner of this once beautiful cottage seemed unable to employ and retain labourers to maintain his property and it gradually slunk into a dishevelled and slatternly appearance.

The English painter who owned Glyndŵr is the same one who used to sell his paintings for £50 in a Cornish market, but now that he has racheted up his style from the local views for tourists, which his mother continues to paint and sell at the Cornish market, and turned to abstract depictions, his price tickets may be multiplied by twenty times the original figure.

Nevertheless, whatever his command of money, he had no command of the local labour force and when the wind lifted slates from his roof and his ceiling sprung a leak, and his stone garden wall tumbled down in disarray just as if a hulking great tractor had hit it on the way down the track, he was compelled to fetch someone all the way from England to fix the damage. This proved unsatisfactory as the English builder vanished with the money before completing the work. The artist found it easier to mend the wall himself rather than let the brickies have another go.

The English man's planning applications for an extension were all rejected. He may have found it helpful to fraternise with the locals or get to know someone on the council, but the thought never occurred to the artist who was too wrapped up in his abstractions. In the end it was more convenient for him to sell the cottage than to keep it.

The next owners of the holiday home proved to be equally at the mercy of external forces. The new member of the community who had bought a holiday home along with her husband which became their second home, their first being in Belgium, had unluckily become confused about the varieties of mushrooms growing in the locality.

The means by which the wicked Agrippina, wife of the august Roman Emperor Claudius, poisoned her husband with a plate of mushrooms has been faithfully recorded by historians. In the case of that perfidious wife however, it seems that she added poison to the mushrooms since the Emperor was a well-known lover and connoisseur of

114

mushrooms and would have been unlikely to have swallowed a variety of poisonous mushroom by mistake.

In this unfortunate case of the holiday home mushroom poisoning, it seems to be a much more straightforward case of a wife mistaking an inedible kind of mushroom for one of the parasol mushrooms which grow around here and are quite common. The woman perhaps did not know the secret of the parasol mushroom, which is to check for the ring underneath the parasol and to push it up and down as if opening a lady's parasol. Just as the ring on a real parasol which is working properly will move up and down quite freely, so the ring under the mushroom umbrella should move easily up and down the stem. If not it should be discarded at all costs.

Luckily in this case the victim survived the dose of bad mushrooms and, after an unpleasant period with agonising stomach pains, recovered. But he did not recover his initial enthusiasm for the splendid views and unparalleled vista of the sea from Glyndŵr's terrace. The poisoning seemed to have driven it away.

And so Glyndŵr fell into yet another foreigner's hands. It was a short time after the London couple moved in for the summer that an old footpath, which had lain unused and dormant for some years, was suddenly rediscovered on an old parish map. In the spirit of the right to roam and access to ancient footpaths, Mr Rees-Jones and Mr Preece-Williams of the local walking club took to marching up and down this footpath at all hours of the day and night and sticking yellow footpath labels and indicators on the gateposts, for the benefit of other ramblers and so that yet another footpath across this holy isle should not be lost to walkers in the future.

The footpath took a rather unusual route through the two acre garden of Glyndŵr and wended its way between the house and its detached garage and up into the field behind, which overlooked Glyndŵr's back garden. If the walkers happened to be facing in the direction of the house as they ascended the path towards the field they would automatically glance straight into the owners' windows.

Once this ancient path had been recovered it was used with enthusiasm by an increasing number of ramblers, led to the spot by the arrows and footpath signs left by Mr Rees-Jones and Mr Preece-Williams, and by the eulogies of those two ramblers on the subject of the views which could be had over to the Snowdon mountains and the Lleyn Peninsula.

The London owners were furious, complaining of unwarranted intrusion on their privacy and of persecution, and most unreasonably demanding closure of the footpath. However it is my conviction that the true source of their anger lay in the drop in value of their investment. Whatever sum they had bought the house for could not possibly be realised on resale now that the property had a thoroughfare running slap bang through the middle of it. The adage *buyer beware* is a good one, and at no time is this more true than when one is attempting to buy into a foreign culture with its own language and customs and ways of doing things.

CHAPTER 16

FISH & CHIPS AND
LOTTERY WINNERS

List of contents:-
How a bird stole my fish.
An unpleasant stench when the vicar arrives.
The problems of septic tanks.
The salt cellar levitates and upsets the vicar.
I wrecked the vicar's punch line.
A superfluity of nuns.

*

There can be no two opinions on the subject of fish and chips. The Dolphin chippy is inarguably the best fish and chip shop on the island. If you want unmatched chips, golden coloured, slightly oily, sticking together, and crisp battered fish, the fryer there is your man. In consideration of which I was furious to be attacked on the footpath to the marina one weekend by a seagull whose object was my crispy orange fish, which I had been looking forward, yes slavering at the chops, to eat.

As I held the wrapper of fish and chips in my hands, walking along, stabbing the golden chips liberally seasoned with salt and vinegar with my blue plastic fork, and with a can of coke ensconced in my coat pocket, I was looking forward to the melt in the mouth moment when I would break open the delicious crispy batter and eat the white fish inside.

As I strolled along the footpath imagining the first bite, sniffing in the smell of fish and chips, a huge white seagull with a yellow beak swooped down and seized my fish with all the dexterity that he no doubt had previously seized things from the waves. To be robbed is one thing. To be robbed of dinner when you have already smelt the incomparable savoury is the most annoying thing in the world. Half of the fish, which was huge to begin with, broke off as the greedy gull seized it and fell on the ground, as the bird rose into the air with the other half as its prize. In consideration of bird flu and possible avian flu pandemics, I was forced to dispose of the remaining chips in one of the litter bins lining the promenade by the bus stop.

On the subject of fish, and food from the water, there was nothing Huw Llewellyn-Jones and his father Dai enjoyed so much as a delicious eel or two, usually cooked upon the barbecue in its own juices since the eel is an oily enough creature not to need an addition of oil to the pan when cooking. Neither is perturbed by Rhodri or Alun's squeals of, "Ugh, snakes," when they see the elongated creatures cooking in the pan.

Anni prefers jellied eels but although the eels are obliging enough to jelly themselves without any help given enough time, in her house with its two eel connoisseurs, the eel delicacy is rarely kept long enough to turn into jelly of its own accord.

When the smell of eels cooking in a pan drifts into neighbouring gardens I always think to myself that had no one coined the collective term for a group of eels, a *fry* of eels would have sprung to mind immediately, so apt does it seem when the cooking smells come floating over the grass.

Gwyneth's choice of delicacy is crab pâté which her mother makes in individual pots of small size for the small girl. The crabby delicacy adorns the table on a certain day of the week at teatime, and Gwyneth has been most vociferous in her complaints on the rare occasions that the pot of crab pâté has not been forthcoming. She looks and sounds plaintive on those occasions as she did when she was two years old and wanted hot chocolate when she woke in the night, instead of the glass of water which was placed on the bedside table in its stead.

"But Mama," she would say, "I'm not feeling for water. I want hot chocolate now."

For myself, I am very partial to crab and could happily eat it seven days of the week, or perhaps six days since I am also partial to my Sunday roast Welsh lamb with mint sauce, hot red cabbage and mashed potato. However there was one unfortunate incident with a crab shell that has slightly dented my preference for that delicious crustacean. It occurred the time that I dined at the local restaurant and chose crab starter.

All well and good because it arrived with its pinky brown shell looking appetising and tasting every bit as good as it looked. I scraped out the inside of the crab shell, extracting every last residue with my spoon and then, noticing that the crab shell was a particularly handsome one and might amuse my niece Eiry who collects shells, I wrapped what remained of the crab inside my napkin and put it in my handbag.

Since I did not pay the bill on that occasion I had no reason to open my handbag again that night and the crab, which had formed the basis of a corking starter, stayed in the bag. I returned from work the following day in the evening to find my partner's father, the vicar, waiting in the car outside the house. Unluckily we were not greeted by his son once I had turned the key in the lock and let us into the hallway, as Martyn was still working, but rather by the most terrific stink I think I had sniffed since the septic tank overflowed its underground chamber and seeped into the garden and down the drive through not having been emptied for three years.

119

I should add that it was not the defecatory habits of myself or dear Martyn that led to the overflow, nor was it our fault that the tank had not been emptied in three years for we had only just taken up residence in our new home, and in fact we had inherited the contents of the septic tank from the previous owners. As Martyn rightly said at the time, when we were forced to walk around holding our noses and watering the garden with the hose pipe in order to disperse the residue, one would have thought that when selling a house, the last thing one should leave behind is one's faecal waste. Of course as it is impossible to take it amongst the luggage, a phone call to the septic tank emptiers is surely in order?

Within the first week of our arrival we were thus forced to the extremity of knocking on our neighbours' door and asking to use their loo. Not at all the first impression one wants to give new neighbours; that one is likely to be asking regularly for a loan of something, let alone their loo. Thankfully the septic tank emptying company, of which there are many listed in the Yellow Pages for Chester and North Wales, were able to come with their truck and long pipe and empty the tank within a day.

But to put an end to this unedifying subject and return to the matter of food, as I was saying, I had no sooner let the vicar over the doorstep than a powerful stench assailed our nostrils. At first I was puzzled to account for it, except in terms of the drains, but then the truth revealed itself when I reached into my evening bag, which was still sitting on the hall table, for a handkerchief to hold over my nose, that the awful and pungent smell came from the rotting crab shell which I had forgotten to wash.

It was one of those irretrievable occasions. No matter what excuse is offered for the vile smell of one's home when one's almost-father-in-law steps over the threshold, one nevertheless creates an indelible impression when there is an odious smell in the air. An attack on the olfactory organs is not easily assuaged. Useless to protest that the house is clean, regularly scrubbed and vacuumed; bootless to claim that it is all the fault of a small oversight, a good deed in saving a crab shell for my young niece's collection.

I have been born with many advantages, I cannot deny it. I am the youngest daughter of a family which has had pure Welsh blood in its veins for seven generations on both sides; I thus have some of the magical qualities that come as birthright to such rare women, however, even I was unable to efface the appalling smell despoiling my handbag and perfuming the house with a smell like ancient rotting fish. Nor was I able to erase the impression it gave to the worthy vicar who, truth to tell, I have had little success in winning over, due to his old fashioned views regarding couples living together without the benefit of a church wedding, and such-like.

It is true also that I have a degree of prescience related to future events thanks to the gifts conferred by Celtic blood, but one did not need to read the tea leaves to divine that the vicar considered it an attack on his professional standards to have his own son living with someone outside the sacred channels of grace and the sacrament of marriage.

If I must be truthful, I should confess that there was another circumstance which led the vicar into regarding me as something of a light-minded character, and this happened to take place when I was first introduced to the vicar's social circle at a dinner party held by the vicar for his friends.

Forgetting I wasn't at home, I'd unthinkingly levitated the salt cellar, finding it a bit of a stretch across the table.

"Oops, sorry," I said.

The vicar hated me doing that.

The vicar is fond of telling anecdotes about his own ministry and, being high church inclined, he was relating a story over dinner about how he had attended the deathbed of a, "Womanising, alcoholic, good for nothing," as the vicar put it, and tried to urge a sense of repentance on the dying man. After trying unsuccessfully to persuade the man to confess and be absolved of his sins, he had to listen to the reprobate saying, "I won't offer my last few hours, the mere dog-end of my days, to God now, hoping to buy heaven, when I have spent the best of them on myself."

At this point I broke in and applauded the nobility of the dying man's sentiment and his refusal to be a hypocrite. However, it seems I had spoiled the vicar's punch line, which was that he had stared hard at the human being fading before him and told him that he was taking a good look because he had never, "Until now looked into the eyes of someone who was going to hell."

I could hear the loud swallow, at my left elbow, of Martyn's wine slipping down his throat as the table went quiet. Whether it was that gulp or the excellency of the wine that makes me remember it was a wonderful Cloudy Bay sauvignon blanc I am never quite sure; or possibly it was my cold certainty that the vicar, who I am told rather fancied the acting profession before he decided to train for the church, had saved up his anecdote to go with the wine that made it memorable.

On the subject of clerics, albeit a now unfrocked one, it is true to say that Fr Tristan's interest in food has increased since his conversation with the bishop over the phone when he was rebuked for wasting the Lord's coins. The numbers on his lottery ticket that day bore a striking similarity to the ones in the newspaper. Such a similarity in fact that the priest had to fetch his reading glasses and call Sister Glenys before he could trust himself to believe his eyes.

There can be few priests lucky enough to have won the lottery, possibly due of course to their not generally buying tickets for what is, after all, a form of gambling. But the priest found himself comfortably independent of financial worries, of the need to work, and of his taskmaster the bishop. Having offered his resignation, he left the priesthood taking the religious sister with him. Sister Glenys who had been deputed by the bishop initially to look after the nervous priest did not default in her duties now. They set up home together in a country retreat on Anglesey and Sister Glenys opened a tea rooms, selling cream teas, Welsh scones and jam, and Welsh cakes, all the delicious comestibles with which she had been feeding Father Tristan for the last seven years.

The collective noun for a group of nuns apparently being a *superfluity*, though I could hardly give this credence if I had not seen the term written down in a book with my own eyes, it could now be said that Sister Glenys was no longer part of the superfluity of her religious order.

It was discovered that Sister Glenys had a lovely mop of dark hair under her veil once she had discarded it. This was not news to Father Tristan who had seen under the veil before, but it was a topic of conversation for everyone else.

News of the lottery ticket winner spread over the isle, carried by the black hairy feet and spinnerets of the gossip-mongering spider and the efficient newsvine by which events were usually carried. Sister Glenys had the advantage when she started up the tea rooms of queues of tourists and island locals who had merely come hoping to catch a glimpse of the lucky lottery winner and possibly shaking his hand, but who ended up staying for cream tea or bara brith.

CHAPTER 17

A TOUR OF ANGLESEY

List of contents:-
The man who never stops digging.
On provoking road rage.
The best sweetie shop on the island.
The place to go if you're looking for a house.
The tragedy of the oyster beds.
Why Holyhead is too heavy and the necessity of depositing heavy weights and sandbags at Beaumaris as a counterbalance.
The anguished commuters are like a flock of starlings.
Boxer shorts on the dual carriageway.
The history of lawn mowers.
The pie-eyed Yorkshire man's beer gate.
The necessity of Wellington boots or long legs.
The last time the Menai Bridge broke was in 1839, and the requirement for fat passengers to walk across.
The Menai Bridge should be boiled in wine.

*

As any motorist knows who regularly drives the A5025 in the direction of Valley, there is a road sign, consisting of a red triangle with a black figure on a white background digging up the road, which very often appears at the road side. I always feel sorry for this black figure because he seems to be continuously at work with little respite. The heap of debris which he's standing over with his shovel and bent back seems never to go down. He appears to be making no impact on his pile of rubble. And he appears so very often on that particular stretch of road that I have often toyed with the idea of making a complaint to the highways department of the council and suggesting that they should give the man a rest. In fact I feel very sorry for that little man with his bent back so constantly toiling away at his heap of dirt.

I am sometimes tempted to pull over onto the grass verge and take my black marker pen out of the glove compartment, and draw a bead of sweat dripping from the labourer's brow in sympathy. I keep my marker pen, along with a bar of chocolate, a loose envelope and stamps, a series of cards with café and restaurant opening times, and a corkscrew with combined bottle opener, in my glove compartment for emergencies. And it is surprising how many crises there are in which one or more of these items is needed.

Before I move on, I feel it incumbent on me to mention the driver who regularly drives in front of me when I am enroute to work via the A5025, in case she should happen to pick up this book and benefit by the advice. This particular motorist drives on her merry way at forty miles an hour on the sixty mile an hour sections of the road, and regularly causes the traffic to build up behind. However, when it comes to the thirty mile an hour stretch of road through the village of Llanfachreath the same driver continues at the speed of forty miles an hour, possibly with the idea of outstripping the law-abiding motorists who drive at the speeds indicated on the signs, and making up for those periods of ambling along when a heavy queue of traffic is forming at the rear. If a hint might be accepted, dear driver, that adjusting one's speed to the road is a good thing, it might just save us all from a very bad thing like road rage which will no doubt be provoked by such a manner of driving.

It is not only the same drivers that one is likely to encounter repeatedly on an isle with a relatively small

125

population, but the same walkers too. Being a local I am familiar with a great many people in this vicinity, but there is a man who regularly walks the road towards Valley who may possibly be a new resident of these parts. Thus if anyone can tell me who the good-looking man is on the Valley road who wears a blue anorak, carries a newspaper and a carrier bag, and who resembles Michael Kitchen, I should be very glad to come by the information.

There is also a white haired man who walks daily on a further stretch of that road who uncannily resembles a Time Lord. He appears to get up earlier in the morning than the Michael Kitchen man so that it is unlikely they would meet on the road since they are both walking in the same direction; the Time Lord being two miles in front of Michael Kitchen. If either of them, on reading this, should wish to alter their time for walking, they might find themselves with a companion on their exercise.

If heading in the opposite direction on the A5025, away from Valley into Cemaes high street, one will find the best sweetie shop on the island. The owner has thoughtfully provided little baskets in the sweetie corner to save small hands from overflowing with the sweet things they buy with their pocket money on Saturday mornings. Without those baskets which resemble small versions of the pans that prospectors use when panning for gold, many a toffee or gobstopper would have rolled its way under the display shelves never to be seen again. And the baskets, although smaller than prospectors' pans, are of a large enough size to accommodate the consequences of having a particularly generous parent and plentiful pocket money.

For those requiring a little assistance in purchasing their sweets from the huge variety on offer, I can particularly recommend the white gobstoppers with rainbow coloured speckles scattered over the outer casing, and the old fashioned aniseed balls with a tiny black aniseed in the centre which you get to once you have sucked your way through the outer layers.

It is the gobstoppers, however, that get my vote because they are sufficiently large and hard that they don't crumble too soon. One likes to feel that one has got value for money in having a big bulge in the cheek for a long time before the jaw breaker collapses in your mouth at last. Also there are some modern jaw breakers which contain chewing gum and the sucking time is far less, which I do not approve of at all.

Before I go on with the tour, I should just put in a good word for the treacle toffees in this shop, made in the old way from dark black treacle; and also for the bonfire lollies which are sold around November 5th. The bonfire lollies are just the sort my mother and grandmother used to make, the treacle being poured into small round foil dishes with a lolly stick, so that when one peels off the foil casing, one is left with a lolly in a shape resembling a pastry tart.

And on the left of the high street just before the sweetie shop is Holly's house. Or rather it used to be Holly's house because that unfortunate friend of mine no longer lives there thanks to the plans of RAF commanders who have sent her father to another base somewhere abroad in England, as they used to do with my father almost immediately we had settled into any halfway decent place to live. Farewell Holly who will never again spend your money loading those generously sized baskets with your sweeties bought from the fifty pence you were given on Saturdays.

Down the steps, behind the tea rooms at Cemaes, and along the river walk may be found growing on the trees some of the rare ciliate strap lichen which looks like frosting, and which can only be found on Anglesey and one or two other places in the country.

And then if one is hungry after all one's exertions it might be wise to make a visit to the bakery, also in the high street, and buy oneself an oggie: A rather delightful treat for lunchtime somewhat resembling an oversized Cornish pasty.

For harassed parents needing somewhere to take their offspring on wet weekends, and fed up of being requested to get out of bed in order to relieve the boredom of those unoccupied children whose schools have not given them enough homework, there is no better place than the next stop on our tour – the nuclear power station on the north shore of this lovely isle, where a helpful man called John works, is to be recommended.

Alongside the children's playground where my niece Eiry once had the misfortune to fall and cut her knee when I was minding her, obliging me to ask the power station staff for a plaster, which they happily gave, there is a nature reserve which at its summit boasts marvellous views over the sea.

The forest planted by the power station, consisting mainly of one type of tree, conifers, rather than the broadleaf trees which might attract squirrels or other wildlife, is uncannily quiet and strangely bereft of birds. I imagine that the cause is the recent planting of the trees and the lack of enough time for news to have got around about the conveniently placed bird boxes evidently designed to encourage our feathered friends to move in. I imagine it will merely be a matter of time before the wildlife arrives to inhabit this place altruistically designed for their benefit.

For those who require refreshment after driving across the isle to the nuclear power plant, there is a café on site which I have used on many occasions, frequently receiving my second cup of tea for free after purchasing the first.

Further round the island on the east side is Red Wharf Bay where there is a renowned pub serving delicious food, where certain professional colleagues meet to talk shop at weekends. If one is looking for an out-of-the-way house, a rural retreat in this area, there is no better place to go than at times when the nurses from the hospitals and GPs surgeries meet there for lunch, because there is no bunch of people better placed even than the estate agents to advise you on the purchase of such a place.

At Beaumaris, rightly known as the Welsh Mediterranean for the beauty of its views and its azure coastline, there are mussel and oyster beds for those who, like me, appreciate the traditional occupations of our island fishermen. This may unfortunately be the last time I include the mussel beds on my tour of island geography since this wonder of nature is likely to be swept away in favour of the development of a marina in this ancient town. I am informed that this development is taking place due to symmetry. Geographically Beaumaris is diagonally opposite to Holyhead and I am told that Beaumaris needs a marina as large as Holyhead's in order to balance the isle so that one side does not fall into the sea through being too weighty.

My personal feeling and lament, is that it is a pity no other remedy can be found for the problem of Holyhead being too heavy for sustainability. Why it is not possible to deposit sandbags or heavy weights on the Beaumaris side of the coastline to keep it floating level with Holyhead, thus saving the mussels and oysters, I cannot fathom, but this is why I am not a town planner or an officer of the council, because I lack engineering and environmental nous.

And Holyhead, our magnificent town, of such weight that even the magical stilts which hold it up clear of the sea are buckling, is the place to see the pied-wagtail; that original little bird about the size of a sparrow with its comical jerky movements, rather similar to those wind-up toys you can get in the one pound shop, which run about and eventually wind themselves down to a halt.

The first time you see a wagtail there is no mistaking it for another bird, even if you have not seen a copy of it elsewhere, because of the wagging up and down of its feathered tail. If you are not sure where the island's bird hides are located, the car park of the Ucheldre centre is a good place to look for a wagtail, and a cup of tea may be had into the bargain.

The flocks of starlings inhabiting Anglesey are a joy to behold at any time. With their incessant chattering and twittering, and co-ordinated movements, darting en masse between trees, sweeping from left to right and back again, they resemble a sight I once saw on a London train platform. This being a commuter hour the trains were very full. Once the carriages of a train had begun to overflow with crammed-in commuters, the train would shut its doors, irrespective of whether there were any customers left standing on the platform. The howls of anguish that arose from the passengers left behind on the platform resembled the vociferous twittering of starlings; and the dozens of pairs of feet that ran in unison from the closed doors at the front of the train to the doors at the rear of the train, and back again, in the vain hope that there may yet be an open door through which they could gain admittance to the train and hence to work on time, was a sight to behold.

On this splendid isle we know little of commuting hours and overcrowded trains. The one major road across the isle, the A55, running across the Britannia Bridge and on to the ferry port at Holyhead, is often empty at times for stretches of several miles. On once occasion I was driving to Holyhead for my weekly shopping and was impeded merely by a series of shoes, white shirts and boxer shorts strewn out across the carriageway.

I performed a slalom manoeuvre around them, wondering who could possibly have left their clothes on the road and whether they wouldn't be missing them, when the cause was revealed as I caught up the one car on the dual carriageway with an Irish licence plate which was evidently going hell for leather to catch the boat to Ireland from Holyhead ferry port. The top of his luggage box had blown off in the wind and, further along the road from the clothes, it lay in the road looking for all the world like a small rowing boat stranded at low tide. Either the owner of the clothes had not noticed his luggage box flying off in the wind and scattering his clothes, or he preferred losing the shirt and pants to missing the ferry boat.

Perhaps it was as well the Irishman, as I imagine him to be with his Dublin licence plate, did not stop to retrieve his wardrobe because he may have been obliged to play chicken with the other cars on the road when picking up the shirts which were strewn at intervals on both sides of the crash barrier; and there is no saying he could have recovered them even if he had parked on the hard shoulder because the wind was dispersing them at ever greater distances, over the hedges and walls and into the fields lining the dual carriageway.

One must not forget on this tour, the Yorkshire man's field. Although a foreigner and not a native of this isle, the Yorkshire man's field is worthy of inclusion because around the perimeter of his extended garden one can see the entire history of lawn mowers. The implements for cutting grass, range from a hand-pulled plough, to a variety of push lawnmowers, scythes, and a huge collection of ageing petrol mowers in various states of repair.

Due to the Yorkshire man's philanthropy in putting his antique collection on view to the world, free of charge, for it costs nothing to peer over his hedge and into the field and peruse the history of grass cutting tools, many of the items have begun to rust in the rain and salt winds that come off the sea and hover over his field with the sole mischievous purpose of eroding a bit of our island's history.

The Yorkshire man has a curious tree in his garden which at first sight looks like an advertisement or shop window for light shades. At a distance, on my first occasion of seeing them, I had mistaken them for Chinese lanterns but they are in fact a collection, probably the biggest in the world, of bird feeders in all kinds of weird and wonderful shapes and sizes: spheres, cylinders, hexagons, octagons.

It may be that, if you were to knock on the Yorkshire man's door and ask for a guided tour of his little field museum, he would willingly give it, because there is hardly a more good-natured man on the isle; and it may be that he would even allow you to use his beer gate which is the nearest entrance from the road into the field. The beer gate so called because it is conveniently placed for access to the local pub and saves the Yorkshire man a longer walk up the track to his official gateway when he is *pie-eyed* as the expression is in Yorkshire for a man who has drunk so much that he is glad for a shorter route home in the evening.

Strangely enough, for a man who owns such a large collection of machines designed for hewing the grass, the Yorkshire man never employs any of his collection in the cropping of his field. In order to save himself the effort of mowing such a large green space, he employs the services of a number of local sheep kindly loaned for the task by a nearby farmer.

The sheep, normally resident in a field further down the track, trot along the road and into the Yorkshire man's field when required for grass cutting duties. Sometimes I have been caught behind those sheep on their return journey to the farmer's field, walking three abreast along the road, unperturbed by the sounds of revving engines or peeping horns. As they trot side by side, like gunslingers in the road, one is forced to wait behind them, inching along in the car for a third of a mile until they have reached their own field again.

For those with a turn for the outdoor life, a trip to Newborough Forest is to be recommended. The convenience of the bird hides for observing rare birds is worth a mention. However, for those making this a family outing, please remember to turn right when arriving at the beach beyond the forest, and not left. Unfortunately the left hand stretch of this lovely beach having been listed on certain adult websites, which are outside the scope of this family work to mention, to the dismay and outrage of native Newboroughites, it is wise to remember to take the right hand turn for an incomparable family day out.

What happens in the sand dunes to the left is none of our concern on this tour; and I sympathise wholeheartedly with those locals who are conducting a campaign to be rid of the antisocial behaviour which takes place at the other end of the beach.

For those with any little difficulties in affairs of the heart, a pilgrimage to St Dwynwen's island offers a solution. The patron saint of lovers, she may be consulted, like an oracle, for those concerned about whether their spouse or their intended will prove faithful. The great fourteenth century Welsh poet Dafydd ap Gwilym prescribed a visit to her island as a remedy for heartache, writing that, "Neither disease nor sorrowful countenance will follow a man from Llanddwyn." Any visitor without Wellington boots or with short legs is advised to cross to the island at low tide.

If one has the stamina for a more challenging walk, I personally recommend the walk from Cemaes, the northernmost point of Anglesey, around to Church Bay. The distance when travelling by car along the road between those two points is about six miles, however, it is considerably further when winding around the coastline on footpaths and this should be borne in mind when making preparations for the walk.

The first time I made this journey in company with a friend, we unfortunately left our water bottles in the car at Cemaes Bay but did not discover what we had done until we were halfway along the route. By this point one is committed to finishing the journey, however thirsty or unwilling, and no matter how one's legs and shins ache, because one is as near to the end of the route as one is to the beginning.

With no shops at which to buy water, or houses at which to beg for it, no roads or public transport where one could throw in the towel and get the bus home, no public telephones from which to phone one's friends to plead for rescue from bodily fatigue and thirst, and no mobile phone signal due to cliffs and the remoteness of the coastal path, one may find oneself in a very unpleasant situation.

And this is the situation in which my friend and I found ourselves without water on a hot summer day with half a day's walk behind us and half a day's walking in front of us. It was one of those horrific situations of which the poet Coleridge rightly says, *Water water everywhere nor any drop to drink*. Stretched out before us were some of the most wondrous views of nature that one may contemplate anywhere in the world, utter isolation, blue sea for miles and miles to the horizon, and no water to drink.

If any drink had been to hand to quench my parched throat that time, I would have appreciated the sea views, the vivid blue butterflies on the coastal path between Cemaes and Cemlyn Bay – the Common Blue is readily seen here as its name suggests; the sight of the Skerries lighthouse close up; the natural rock arch near Llanfairghornwy, but as it was we had to keep going like dogs with our tongues hanging out in search of water.

Having looked after many dogs during my life, I know that dogs are willing to take water from almost anywhere if they are thirsty, any stagnant pond, no matter how ill-smelling or repugnant it may seem to its owner. I have met dogs that preferred water a day, or even two days old, rather than fresh. I even looked after one dog for a friend when she was on holiday, who preferred drinking out of the toilet bowl to anything else. I had to ensure that anyone who used the loo flushed it immediately afterwards of course, because this dog (like dung-eating beetles) definitely had coprophagous tendencies.

In the course of our waterless hike, my friend and I eyed one or two mountain streams which cut their way across our path and trickled down to the sea, with a view to drinking, but when we looked upstream we saw that they were well trodden with hoof prints and contaminated with cow pats and sheep droppings. As neither of us had coprophagous tendencies we could not bring ourselves to resort to doggy behaviour and drink the filthy water.

We met no one on our walk until well past the halfway point as very few people attempt the whole walk. I was quite prepared to mug the first pair of walkers we met on the cliffs at Mynachdy for their water, but when the hospitable pair realised our waterless plight they kindly offered us their spare water bottle rendering a snatch unnecessary.

Once I had quenched my thirst, I was able to think sensibly again and it occurred to me to wonder about those lovely birds, the black and white feathered oyster catchers with orange beaks which may be seen along the stretch of coast here. Seeing that the collective noun for a group of oysters is a *bed*, I wondered whether an oyster catcher bird could be thought of as seizing a bed if he caught more than one oyster at a time?

Just as the Tylwyth Teg never leave their own locality, my nephew, Dylan Jones's worst thing is crossing the bridge to the mainland. He once saw a television programme in which a suspension bridge undulated in the wind and cracked its road surface. He is terrified that one day the Menai Suspension Bridge is going to collapse under the weight of heavy traffic and it may be on the very occasion when he is travelling across it. My nephew is never happy until he is back on the island again.

In vain I reassure him that the last time the road broke in the wind was in 1839 and that the bridge has undergone improvements in its construction since, and an increase in its weight-bearing capacity. It has stood for many years without mishap and the days when bus conductors had to ask certain passengers to descend and walk across the bridge, to lighten the load of the bus, are long gone.

How they chose which passengers should ride and which should cross the bridge on foot in those pre-political correctness days I have not been able to find out. Whether it was totally based on weight considerations, the girth of one's belly, or whether they had regard to age, infirmity or gender in deciding who to eject from their seats I do not know.

The White Knight in *Through the Looking Glass* tells Alice that he had completed a design, "To Keep the Menai Bridge from rust. By boiling it in wine."

So far as I can ascertain, the iron chains were never boiled in wine although I understand that Thomas Telford had them boiled in warm linseed oil to preserve them, but it seems no more preposterous a suggestion to boil a bridge in wine than it does to hang a road up on chains across a vast chasm with a huge drop below it.

I mention my nephew's favourite spot on the island because whenever he returns home from a journey off the isle he looks immediately for the tall column on which stands a statue of the Marquis of Anglesey and points it out for all the world as though he were a tour guide. He considers the height of the marquis's column to be a mark of that gentleman's importance in our nation's history, clearly far more important than the fellow on the little stone pedestal somewhat below the marquis on the bank of the Menai Strait who goes by the name of the Duke of Wellington. The duke is also somewhat dwarfed by the grandeur of the massive stone lions at either end of the Britannia Bridge which are easiest to see by boat from below, as one cannot see them from the car when crossing the bridge, unless you find somewhere to park and peer over the parapet.

Grand as they are, standing four metres high, with another four metres of plinth, the lions have taken a step down in life from their former elevated position guarding the portals of the Britannia Bridge. They appear rather forlorn having been demoted from keepers of the Britannia to a position below road level.

CHAPTER 18

A BRIEF HISTORY OF YNYS MÔN

List of contents:-
An Anglesey pirate turned lighthouse keeper.
The story of a broken heart.
A death caused by blackout curtains.
A politically incorrect gravestone and how it was banned.
How Aunt Mererid lost her voice and how it came back
again.
Aunt Mererid is caught unawares by death.
Rex Whistler - a famous victim of a broken heart.
The naked aristocrat and the Marquis of Anglesey's rude
dining room.
Alfred Tennyson's trip to Wales.
How the Greeks are nicer than the Romans.
How Tennyson mistook Welsh women's hats for beavers.
Aberffraw – the capital of broken hearts.
The story of Branwen and a good for nothing husband.
The Welsh hero Bran cops it from the in-laws.
The magic talking head with no body.
(Apologies for the length of the chapter but an interesting
history necessitates a longer chapter)

*

There are too many histories of this fair isle, with which I
could not possibly compete, for me to give more than a few
hints and a brief overview of one or two noteworthy events
and people in its history.

The surplus of wrecks around the Anglesey coast testifies to the necessity of this island's network of lighthouses and beacons.

It may interest the reader to know that a Mr Robert Beavor from Aberffraw was the first lighthouse keeper at Point Lynas lighthouse on north east Anglesey. How many Anglesey pirates there have been over the generations it is impossible to ascertain but it seems certain that Mr Beavor was a member of that exciting profession; and that while he was engaged at one end of the sea in capturing ships in the West Indies, at the other end he was occupied in saving ships from foundering on the treacherous rocks of Anglesey. An early example of a multi-tasker, he died in 1814 and was buried in Llaneilian churchyard.

My Aunt Mererid who died of a broken heart when her husband left her for a younger woman was also a native of Aberffraw.

Sometimes one hears the beginning of a story thinking that it preludes great things, the story of a hero. Thus it was once with a story I heard some time ago in a nursing home where an old lady told me about her brother who died in the war. I waited to hear tales of great deeds, or at least of battlefields, guns and tanks. But the brother had died in the war due to the blackout curtains it seemed. Puzzled as to how curtains could cause a death I listened for the remainder of the tale which was that, due to the need to pull the blackout curtains, her brother had to change a light bulb in the dark. He missed his step, fell between two chairs and broke his neck while changing the bulb. And that was the extent of her brother's war and the end of his life.

My aunt's story is something the same as this gentleman's. It sounds a grand thing to die of a broken heart. One envisages Romeo and Juliet, Dido casting herself on a funeral pyre, but the grand fact may hide details which, when laid bare, form the basis of a sad and sorry tale rather than a grand tragedy.

Her brother fell foul of the authority that decides which epitaphs are appropriate for headstones in public places. "Died of a broken heart," was deemed too political an epitaph and indeed to indicate some degree of blame to an unspecified person. Mr Jones endeavoured to persuade the authorities that Mererid might just as well have died from a broken heart over her deceased dog as over the absent husband, but this appeal on behalf of the headstone was disallowed. Since doctors and coroners do not record broken hearts as causes of death, it was officially attributed to pneumonia with complications. And the *complications* had to satisfy Mr Jones as a vague explanation for heartbreak due to desertion.

However in our family the cause of Mererid's death is always acknowledged to be a failure of the heart to recover from abandonment. It is said in countries with a sceptical mindset that no one dies any longer of a broken heart; but here in our Celtic nation where we understand music and stories and hearts, we have a greater wisdom.

My Aunt Mererid, before she died of her broken heart, suffered terribly from nerves and anxiety. As a child she had refused to stay in bed at nights, and her mother would wake up in the morning to find Mererid curled up in the armchair, in the dog's bed, and once in the monk's seat in the hall with the lid down and in danger of suffocation. To stop the little girl wandering at night, her mother placed a black crow's feather on Mererid's pillow when she went to bed, warning her that if she got out of bed or put so much as a foot on the ground before morning, the Crowman would come to get her.

Petrified, the little girl lay pinioned to the bed, stiff like a cadaver, hardly daring to breathe, with the crow's feather on the pillow beside her. Ever since then, poor Mererid had been terrified of both feathers and birds. Sometimes when she used to take me out if my mother was busy, I had to run in front of her, chasing away any birds that came too near.

Even once she married she was unable to go to the toilet by herself in the middle of the night and suffered nightmares about the terrible black Crowman depicted in her mother's stories.

During one summer when clearing the gutter of debris, her husband dislodged an old bird's nest lined with feathers which fell down on Mererid who was holding the ladder beneath. The shock drove Mererid's voice away completely for two years. After two years it began to come back again but it always sounded slightly cracked from shock ever after.

My unfortunate aunt suffered from a succession of unpleasant encounters with birds in her relatively short life. One time when I was returning with her in the car from the dentist, a fat male pheasant with vibrant feathers shot out of the hedge and straight into the path of the car. Not for nothing is the collective noun for a group of fowl a *plump* of fowl. The pheasants of Anglesey are as fat as any pheasants I've seen anywhere, which may be due to their lazy lifestyle and lack of anxiety since nobody tries to shoot them.

There was no time to avoid the bird and I waited for the sickening bump and crunch that should come as we went over the fat fowl. By some miracle the pheasant escaped the wheels of the car and emerged at the side of the road unharmed though indignant. Poor Mererid, however, had fainted away even before the bird had disappeared under the chassis.

And then there was the time when she had gone to visit an elderly relative of ours in mid Wales and had gone to bed, only to wake in the night and find there was a tiny hole in the pillow and that it was leaking feathers. Although this did not entirely drive away her voice again, it reduced it to a stutter which always intensified when in the presence of birds or feathers. Unfortunately it was impossible to keep feathered creatures entirely at bay. Although she would go to no houses where birds were kept, and there was a scarecrow in her garden, it was not possible to keep my aunt hermetically sealed away from birds.

When I telephoned Mererid's husband in the month before her fortieth birthday to suggest a big family party for Mererid's fortieth he said, "Mererid's birthday isn't 'til next month. But you know whose birthday is next week on Thursday, don't you?"

I scanned my calendar pinned up next to the phone, alarmed that I'd forgotten a family birthday, although I'm usually meticulous about special occasions and anniversaries, and finally I had to say I'd forgotten whose birthday it was.

"It's Glenda's birthday," he said.

I couldn't think of anyone I knew called Glenda.

"Glenda, my secretary."

I couldn't think when I'd met Glenda the secretary but since Mererid's husband obviously expected me to know when her birthday was, I dutifully offered birthday wishes for Glenda.

There are times in life when you hear something that seems insignificant or irrelevant that later turns out to be a very big thing. This was one of those occasions. Glenda's birthday is as memorable to me as my own mother's, or Mererid's, since that is the date when Mererid's husband left her to set up home with Glenda.

The strange thing about death is that this event which puts an end to one's hopes, dreams and ambitions, all that one has, is often not dramatic when it comes. Sometimes it steals up on a person quietly, in a creep mouse kind of way, unexpectedly. You look at a deceased person's face, with their soul now gone, and wonder if they saw it coming. And probably they didn't. They were caught unawares, just like my Aunt Mererid who was a rather dignified woman and would hardly have been caught short in the position she was found in, if she had had an inkling that death was going to come at that moment.

141

She was found sitting on the loo and because she had obviously been sitting there for some time she had gone stiff in a sitting position. When they lifted her, they had to form a chair with hands underneath to carry her from the toilet seat. Whatever was remaining of a motion only half-passed now dropped, through sheer force of gravity as they raised her, into the toilet bowl. The two grown men, hearing the splash, dropped Aunt Mererid in terror and hotfooted it from the bathroom before realising their mistake and returning to continue their task.

Mererid's legs were still raised and bent from growing cold in a seated position and when they laid her on the bed they tried to force her legs down flat, but the deceased lady merely kept sitting up in bed when they put the legs flat. Oh the indignity of death, and the waste, as one more unique perspective and vision shuts on the universe. And for all the thousands of eyes opening afresh on the world there will never be another pair exactly the same.

On the subject of broken hearts, a more famous victim of this merciless malady than my poor dear aunt was the painter, Rex Whistler, whose 58 feet of canvas containing a beautiful mural adorns the long wall of the dining room at Plas Newydd, home of the Marquis of Anglesey on the banks of the Menai Strait.

The artist suffered the pangs of love for Lady Caroline, sister to the marquis and included a nude painting of her in the said mural; though it has always puzzled me, I must confess, as to how the artist persuaded the then unmarried aristocratic lady to pose naked for him in an age which was much more decorous than our own, and whether her brother the marquis minded looking at his naked sister on the wall over dinner, or her being on view to the whole world. I know that when my half-sister Olwen did some nude modelling for extra cash as a student, she was very keen not to have it known by the rest of the family and made me promise not to tell anyone.

It will not escape the viewer's notice when examining the mural, that the marquis's rather well-fed dog Cheekie is lolling on a luxurious pink cushion to the right of the picture, leaving untouched his bowl of stew which has been served to him in a grand bowl that looks as though it might have come from the dining room. Possibly the marquis's family did not object to sharing their plates and dishes with the family pet? The dog would appear rather spoilt since he has wasted his stew at a time of national austerity and rationing during the war years.

It may also elicit concern in the spectator's mind that some member of the family, or possibly Whistler himself, has left a cigarette burning on the floor close to the dog. I believe this would nowadays be considered most unwise and might result in a visit from an organisation dedicated to the welfare of animals.

Given the prevalence of anti-smoking sentiment in today's society and in the media, one might almost venture to suggest that the cigarette could be painted out of the picture as being injurious to public health and surplus to requirements, in the same way that the marquis himself asked Whistler to remove one of the tall ships from his mural because the scene was apparently too cluttered.

Whistler complied with the demands of his fine art critic and painted over the tall ship, substituting instead a tall tower with scaffolding. He informed his aristocratic patron that the scaffolding was a precaution should the marquis require him to take the tower down the following day.

It is asserted in the history books that Whistler died at age 39 in Normandy, on his first day of service in the war. My own personal feeling, knowing something of these matters because of my poor Aunt Mererid, is that it was the old heart that did for him. But as I have before mentioned, these maladies of the heart do not find their way into history books and official sources.

For those given to mysteries it might occur to wonder who has left their glasses with the lenses face down on the ground close to the dog, with the certainty of their being scratched on the stone terrace even should no one tread on them, and to ask who has carelessly walked into the marquis's house with bare feet, leaving a trail of wet footprints as they did so?

Unless of course the figure of Neptune the sea god, whose wet foot prints they appear to be, is intended to represent the marquis himself, in which case he is perfectly entitled to tread upon his own carpets with sodden feet. Clearly the household was rich enough not to care about the effects of salty seawater on carpets which I have found to be the very worst thing of all. It takes only a few occasions of padding over carpet with salty wet feet to observe a trail of footmarks on the carpet where the colour is patchy and faded compared with areas of carpet that have remained untrodden.

When I mentioned my worries about permanent trails of footprints and faded carpets in the marquis's stately home, which I could see from the painting was a dead cert, to Martyn, he patted my arm and said, "Don't take it to heart," which is exactly what I wanted to say to those young women standing in the market place at Llangefni when I was waiting behind them to purchase my loo rolls. I didn't want to go anywhere else to buy them since this stall is the cheapest place I know of for toilet tissue, but the four women in front of me were discussing *EastEnders* with the stallholder so earnestly that I feared I would never be able to pay for them.

The young women were discussing the behaviour of one of the characters in the soap and telling each other what she should do about her boyfriend of whom they didn't approve. I tried telling the girls that they shouldn't take it so seriously – that it was only a TV programme and not real, but this met with such contempt that I had to put the loo

144

rolls back and slink off to the chemist because it seemed I had no chance of being served before lunchtime. Whether the soap lady ever took the advice of the girls about her boyfriend I do not know.

Mr Whistler it seems was fond of Anglesey and of the marquis's home on the banks of our fair isle, which is more than can be said for Mr Alfred Tennyson who apparently found nothing in Wales to make his journey worthwhile when he travelled up from London. Admittedly he was speaking of Aberystwyth, a place to which I have never been, since I avoid leaving my island home if at all possible. Not only do the magical properties of the isle disappear at the bridge as if ordered to disperse by some genie, but so do any of those prophetical gifts belonging to the female line of Welsh Celts.

If Mr Tennyson had travelled further north, he would have found plenty to surprise and interest him, just as Lewis Carroll did when he went on holiday and found the rabbit hole in Llandudno (which Alice fell down) and Wonderland at the bottom of it.

I am sure that Tennyson, like Carroll, could have had wonderful adventures and excitement if he had bothered to travel on a little further; just as those ancient Romans did when they lined the banks on the far side of the Menai Strait and caught their first glimpse of our island inhabitants and its magnificent and fearsome Druids, along with the naked women who pranced about with terrifying yells and struck fear into the hearts of those unprincipled conquerors who spilled the finest blood of our isle and desecrated its sacred druidic oak groves.

The ancient Greeks were a far nicer people than the ancient Romans, much more akin to the Celtic spirit with their love of poetry, song and dance. And if, as that old rogue Herodotus commented of himself in his own histories, one cannot help but stop to digress and gather flowers while in the business of telling a history, it is simply because the

145

history of such a people is necessarily so interesting that it refuses to go into the proper channels and insists on winding about.

We forgive Mr Tennyson on the grounds that he did not extend his trip far enough north to overcome his prejudices and for his own rather splendid poetry; and at least it can be said of him that he did admire the pretty faces of young women he found on his Welsh tour, even though he made the ridiculous mistake of confusing the Welsh hats they were wearing with men's hats – men's top hats or *beavers* as he referred to them. I suppose it did not occur to his Welsh hosts, who are notoriously polite and well-mannered to other races, to ask Mr Tennyson why he was wearing a Welsh woman's hat since it is entirely clear to those of us in the north that our delightful top hats and beavers quite obviously suit pretty girls more than bearded, aged men.

Mr Tennyson never had the good fortune to cross the Angle Sea to this fair isle, where for many years the capital of North Wales was based at none other than Aberffraw, ancestral seat of the princes of Gwynedd, and home to Mr Robert Beavor the Point Lynas lighthouse keeper, as well as Aunt Mererid. Aberffraw also lays claim to be the capital of broken hearts for it is in this place, on the banks of the River Alaw, that Branwen, sister of Bran, lies buried after her heart broke in her body. The spot of her burial being known as Ynys Bronwen (The Isle of Bronwen).

The story of Branwen is already famous across the world because of its place in the *Mabinogion*. She married Matholwch from Ireland in a splendid ceremony held at Aberffraw in a silk tent. Branwen's brother, Bran, was a man of such large stature as used to inhabit this sacred isle, that he could not fit into any house or building. It was necessary for him to carry a tent wherever he went for protection from the elements since there was not a dwelling that could contain him.

146

Tragically, Matholwch, the man of Ireland, turned out, like so many of the scoundrels, not to be a good husband; treating his wife Branwen badly once he returned with her to Ireland and she was away from the aid and succour of her family, getting his servants to box her ears because he was often too tired to knock her about himself. After a time Branwen was obliged to send for her brother to come and sort out her husband.

The huge Welshman was forced to wade to Ireland, being too big to go in a ship. He arrived in a bit of a chip due to wet feet and sodden clothes, and a fight broke out with the in-laws which got out of hand. One or two people were killed but fortunately the Welshman carried a stock of Celtic magic about with him in the form of a cauldron which could resurrect the dead, and once the drunken brawlers had been thrown into the pot and brought back to life a semblance of order was restored.

Unfortunately during the fight, our hero, the giant Welshman, the like of whose stature has never been seen since, copped it by way of a poisoned spear in his ankle. Like all true Celts, our Bran was so distraught at the thought that he would never be able to talk again or see his home, he got his friends to cut off his head and carry it back to this fair isle. Such is the power of the magic air of his Celtic homeland, he was able to keep on talking and eating for eighty years after his death, or at least his head was since they left the body in Ireland.

No doubt the bearers of Aunt Mererid's body thought that something similar had occurred to Mererid when she appeared to be going to the toilet some hours after her death, however, this is getting off the point, which is the story leading up to Branwen's death by broken heart. Once the poor girl had no husband and no brother left, her heart burst open on the banks of the River Alaw and she was laid to rest in the spot where she had fallen to the earth and died from grief.

The friends of Bran continued with his head towards London where it was buried under the white mount, now the site of the Tower of London. Bran being Welsh for raven, and Branwen being Welsh for white raven, it will immediately be seen why there are ravens protecting the Tower of London. Thus it is truly said that a Welshman protects the kingdoms of England and Wales since, as the legend goes, the country is safe only while the ravens stay and protect the Tower of London. So it ill-behoved Mr Tennyson the poet to scoff at the sacred ground he was treading on when he left London for the Welsh marches, since it was a Welshman who stood like a shield ensuring the safety of his country and the poet's home in London.

CHAPTER 19

SMUCKS, SMACKS AND STINGS

List of contents:-

*

My grandfather Aneurin had a temper as black as his Welsh hair. He taught my father and my brothers to row and to fish. He would not take me out in the boat because he said girls could not row, but I was not sorry about this because I could hear his big booming voice over the water, when I stood on the shore watching the boys, and hear him bellowing, "Christ, boy, row. ROW."

One time he took the boys fishing in the rowing boat at Trearddur Bay when a smuck of jellyfish arrived. They were only small ones, about the size of tea cups, almost transparent but pulsating with rainbow colours. When Rhys saw them floating in the water like an army of tiny translucent umbrellas he screamed because he was swimming out of the boat, trying to loosen a fishing line which had got stuck. From the rocks where I was sitting I could hear grandfather shouting, "Christ, swim boy. SWIM."

When we got home at night Rhys started arguing with me about whether it was a smuck of jellyfish which I liked better, or a smack of jellyfish which he liked better. He said smack sounded like the sort of smack or sting you'd get

149

from a jellyfish if it stung you. I said that if that was the case, a group of jellies should be called a sting then, but as nobody had thought to call them a sting of jellyfish, a smuck sounded much nicer.

Sometimes grandfather would take us out for a ride in his old car on Sundays when we were growing up, and when we got lost in the back roads around North Wales he would stop the car in the middle of the road, uncaring whether or not there was any space for cars to pass, and send me or one of the boys into the village shop to ask where we were. I hated being the one picked on for that task but I never dared refuse my grandfather who had the biggest voice I'd ever heard.

He started driving at a time when there were no roundabouts and he never saw the point of them. Instead of going around the roundabout and, "Wasting my tyre rubber," as he put it, he would just drive straight over the top and you would feel the bump of the kerb as he went up and the bump of the kerb as he drove off at the other side.

One time he drove straight over an Anglesey village's prize flower roundabout which had been cultivated for a competition and took the heads off all the flowers. This was the occasion that led to him being arrested and made to reapply for his licence since he was so old. They wouldn't give him another licence but he was unrepentant about the flowers, calling it a silly place to put a garden in the middle of the road.

Probably it was a blessing that either he or the car called time because his car was an ancient Rover with a spare wheel behind, on the lid of the boot, which occasionally dropped off and began rolling away down the street. The number of times my grandfather picked that spare wheel out of the gutter I cannot name, but he never lost it. Then there was the bonnet lid which kept flying up in the wind and which one of us children or, more usually, granny herself, had to keep getting out of the car for and slamming it back down with grandfather shouting at us, "Christ. Push. PUSH HARDER."

My grandmother was a mild and submissive woman. Whether she was this way by nature or whether it was the result of years of practice at submission due to my grandfather's having a stronger character I do not know.

There was a time when she had gone shopping at Llangefni market for a new coat and had been talked into trying on a coat which was obviously several sizes too big for her. When she had timidly whispered in the stallholder's ear that she didn't think the coat fitted, he promptly rolled up the sleeves, which had been hanging down below her hands by about a foot in length and said, "Look, it fits now."

I have to say at once that this stallholder was not typical of those normally working on the stalls. By his looks and his accent he was not a local nor even a Welshman, and I only saw him on one occasion. But my poor timid grandmother was ready to part with her money to the hard-nosed market seller, until my grandfather came back from his favourite stall selling tobacco and was barely restrained from putting his hands around the rogue trader's throat.

My grandmother was not a woman to insist on her rights and, like me, she hated being sent into shops by grandfather in order to enquire where we were, if we found ourselves lost on a trip. Once she had been ordered into a Post Office to enquire for directions and to cash a postal order for my granddad. Due to not being known in this strange place, my granny was asked for a form of identification in order to cash the postal order. She was at a loss, not having brought anything in with her, and rather fearful at the time we were taking since grandfather was out in the street honking his horn impatiently.

There were often horns honking. Grandfather was not always careful about where he parked in the street and, even if he was blocking the road, he was reluctant to move until whomever he had sent in to get directions came out again.

151

My granny thought for a moment about the request for ID and finally pointed at me, saying, "I've got my granddaughter, will she do?"

The assistant sighed and told her that I wouldn't do, and that a written form of identification, like a letter, was needed.

At this my grandmother's face lit up and she said that in her car outside she had her address tacked onto the label of her new coat, at the insistence of grandfather, who had been sure that she would leave her coat somewhere and made her put their address inside just in case. I should hasten to add that the new coat was not the same coat as the oversized one she had tried on at Llangefni market, but a true-fitting coat bought some weeks later from the same market.

This form of identification, however, like myself, was deemed inadequate for the purpose because she had written her own address in the coat which apparently didn't prove anything. In order to be acceptable, someone else needed to have written the address.

After another moment's thought my grandmother announced triumphantly that she had, "A dirty postcard," in her handbag. The counter assistant looked shocked at the suggestion. For after all, this was rural Wales. I was a little shocked myself as I could not imagine my grandparents, who were rather straight-laced, carrying rude seaside postcards about with them. I was relieved to see, once grandmother had fished it out from the depths of her bag, that it was a perfectly respectable sea view on the postcard, with a dirty great footprint on the side where the writing went.

The counter assistant looked relieved too for a second as she scanned the back of the postcard but then she sniffily told my granny that she couldn't decipher the writing on the card and therefore couldn't tell whether it was granny's address or not.

I did not think that this conversation between my grandmother and the counter assistant was going at all well,

152

and I could hear a cacophony of hoots and horn blasts from the street where there was clearly a queue of vehicles building up behind granddad's car. I had begun to bite my nails at this point and, truth to tell, I was rather relieved to see my grandfather's huge and irate form pacing in at the door and striding towards the Post Office counter. It did not take long for my grandfather to persuade the assistant to cash his postal order and we were shortly on our way in the car again, with accurate directions for our journey to boot.

Granddad's car was not the worst I've seen. Bryn Davies — the boy whose life is told in pictures across his body — has a car on which the rear doors can't be used at all because they are kept permanently tied shut with rope. The rope stretches across the interior of the back of the car and holds the two doors closed in tension. Access to the rear of the car is via the front door with a squeeze through the gap between the driver's seat and the passenger's seat, then under the rope which acts like a safety barrier for any passengers in the back.

All the doors of Bryn's car, bar the driver's door, were liable to burst open at any minute unless they were tied, with a real danger of the passengers being spewed out onto the highway. One weekday in fact, on returning from the betting shop, Bryn took a left corner so tightly that the front passenger door sprung wide open and swept a poor cat, which was patiently licking its paws and minding its own business at the side of the road, along the pavement.

The cat was shunted some yards along the pavement before Bryn was able to apply the brakes and thus I reckon probably lost, on average, at least two of its lives. I do not know how many of its nine lives that cat had lost previously, but I hope it was not seven or the loss of these two would have made an end to the animal. Fortunately it seemed not to be down to its last life and, having picked up puss and given it a hard shake to ensure it was still alive, Bryn was able to drive on with a clear conscience.

There was nothing wrong with my Aunt Mererid's car except that she was a highly nervous driver and refused to put the car into reverse gear at all. I do not think she had ever reversed the car. She would travel miles in a forwards direction in order to find a return route rather than simply stop and reverse the car. It made parking in car parks sometimes impossible because whatever parking space she chose had to allow for the possibility of her driving out forwards and never backwards.

Unlikely as it may seem to town drivers, who frequently need to perform tight manoeuvres and get into awkward parking spaces which would be impossible without being able to reverse, it is surprising how little one needs to reverse in a sparsely populated country area with relatively few cars, and Mererid somehow contrived to live her life without reversing.

My nephew Dylan Jones loves motor vehicles of all kinds, especially buses. He is particularly delighted to see his own surname written across the paintwork of nearly every bus that he comes across on this part of the island.

"Not that Jones again!" he shouts delightedly when he sees yet another of the green buses or big coaches belonging to that company which shares my nephew's surname. I think that my nephew assumes the bus company is in the family and so it is, in a sort of way, since I can barely think of a family around here in which I cannot name a relative, friend, or some kind of connection.

CHAPTER 20

THE SPOOK HOUSE

List of contents:-
How an infant is exposed in the snow.
An explanation for the Davies's blue noses.
The social habits of bees.
Caressing the computer.
Morwena Davies sees the spook house.
Fluff in the belly button this time and not the honey.
The strange case of an alien abduction.
A tale spun by a spider.
Carries a warning to storytellers.
A medieval punishment and putting people in the stocks.

*

When it was Morgan Davies's turn again to hitch the winter season behind his tractor, the surly black-haired farmer caught the season by the earlobe and twisted it.

"Get on with you then," he growled, and the season resentfully complied, its cold bleached leprosy-like fingers clinging to the back of the tractor. The tractor gave a cough and a sneeze, spluttering into mechanical life. It continued to growl and clear its throat on its route along the highway between farms, the snow advancing at 25 miles per hour so that where there had been iced dew frosting the grass in the morning, there was now white snow all the way to the Sea of Angles.

The Davies's are a hardy breed of farmers. When Morgan Davies's father, Arwel, was a babe in arms, Morgan's grandfather, Dewi, took his infant son out on the pony cart in winter. The babe of four months, swaddled tight in warm clothes and a blanket, slipped out of the back of the old cart onto the snow. There he lay for an hour or more while Dewi Davies made his way to the stable. It was only when Mrs Davies came out from the kitchen to get her son from the cart that the babe's absence was discovered.

While Mrs Davies returned to her baking, Mr Davies trotted back in his pony's hoof prints, scouring the snow for a baby in a blanket. The child was found, lying where he had dropped onto his back in the snow. There was no sound of crying from the prone infant. Fortunately he had been wrapped warmly but the tip of his nose which had been exposed to the air was blue, and maybe accounts for the fact that all the Davies's have a tinge of blue about their noses, especially in winter.

However, an infant can't be exposed to the surly Welsh winter air for an hour or two at a time without suffering some consequences and it has been said that the freezing sojourn outdoors froze the bones of the Davies clan, who all suffer from arthritis and rheumatism in old age, into brittle ice. It also froze the tempers of the Davies's who share a collective icy temperament.

Deep troughs and cliffs of waves were appearing in the sea, and ice balls of two inches in diameter were hitting the roofs of Anglesey citizens at nights. It made Morwena over in her Bangor home across the bridge shiver under her bedcovers during the hours of dark. She had been bred in the Davies school of endurance and did not switch on her heating at nights, no matter how cold the weather. Her grandfather had survived an hour or two in the snow at four months of age and she was of the same stock.

Unlike bees, those social animals who rub their bodies against the hive walls to generate heat and keep the temperature inside the hive warm, it was not possible for the young woman to rub herself on the walls of her bedroom and keep warm. It was easier though when she had someone to curl up with under the covers at night to keep the

156

temperature in the room up, but at present she was between someone's and had to shiver alone in the cold.

It was the sort of weather that led to the clothes drying hard and stiff on the drying rack in her bathroom. When she took a pair of knickers from the clothes airer in the morning, they were so stiff they could almost have stood upright on their own and needed a bit of pulling about and rolling into a ball to soften them up.

When Morwena Davies got to work on Monday morning with a tinge of blue colour at the end of her nose, she found her colleague at her desk first, apparently stroking and patting her laptop.

"What are you doing then? Kinky, no?" Morwena asked Fflur, as the other librarian stroked both sides of the computer, caressed it underneath and gave it a final affectionate jiggle.

"The feet on this computer," her colleague explained. "It's the notebook's only design flaw. I've had two feet drop off already so that it leans on one side. I have to feel underneath before I put it away in the case, to make sure I've still got the other two feet safe."

Morwena saw that indeed it was true. Fflur's computer had lost two feet on one side so that the laptop veered dangerously to one side.

"You look white, apart from your nose," said Fflur. "As if you'd seen a ghost."

Morwena had been the first person this season to experience the new cold weather. Her father had required her help fastening the season behind his tractor because his arthritis had increased on him in the last year. Bryn had been nowhere to be found at the onset of winter. He was engaged in acquiring a further instalment to the story of his life written across his body in tattoos.

In fact Morwena had seen a ghost. On her way through Trearddur Bay she had seen the spook house on the cliff. Unlike the ghost of Ireland on the west side of the isle, the appearance of the spook house at Trearddur Bay usually heralded an event of an unfortunate nature. But Fflur put Morwena's white skin down to her tussle with that fierce pale-visaged season which Morgan Davies was obliged to put through its paces in the repertoire of seasons.

Morwena knew about the bad luck that comes with antagonising the fairy folk and the Celtic land spirits so she said nothing about the spirit house.

I have seen the house myself on two occasions. To my knowledge it only appears in the evenings and in low light, or when the sun is setting behind it over the sea, and it always precedes bad news. It is a vast dark gloomy cavern of a house, with staring rectangles where there should be windows, and dark cloisters.

The ghostly house stands by itself on the cliff, apparently unreachable, surrounded by a moat of black water. If there is a door it is impossible to see because of the density of darkness that appears in oblongs where windows and doors might be. It emits no light or signs of life of any kind, merely a terrifying blackness, and it has become known amongst locals as the *spook house*, so thoroughly has it succeeded in spooking those few people to whom it has appeared.

The ink dried on the latest saga of Bryn's life and a strange tale it told. There was a slightly flattened silver oval tattooed across his midriff and two grey figures with black almond shaped eyes, resembling extra-terrestrial beings carrying surgical instruments, emblazoned either side of his belly button. If he placed his finger in his belly button and twiddled at the fluff and dirt in the hole where his umbilical cord had once been attached, the grey aliens appeared to be waving their instruments in a threatening manner.

A strange tale sprung out of the smoky air in the local pubs which Bryn frequented. An odd tale about abduction and surgical operations carried out by grey aliens with silver instruments, leaving vivid scars and wounds on Bryn's vast sprawling body. There was a new livid scar stretching from a pectoral muscle down to the silver spacecraft tattooed across Bryn's belly. It had been acquired in the night, was all the response that Bryn would make to enquiries about the new scar.

It was however a tale that dropped onto the beer mat from a long silken strand hanging from a silver web on the ceiling of Bryn's local that called time on Bryn's drinking. The tale that stuck to a spider's legs inching its way down from an unswept corner was a colourful one about the mating and cross-breeding of dark haired Welsh Celts and grey hairless extra-terrestrials.

Whether it was the prospect of tattooed aliens or Welsh-speaking bald grey pygmies that appalled one or two of the hot-headed local youths, who knows, but someone obviously decided to call time on Bryn's drinking and his spectacular belly display of the silver craft and little grey men.

It was a Friday night around 11.30 pm, and the tattooed figure was walking home after turning out time, when he was set upon by assailants who were invisible in the dark. The broken nose and two black eyes sustained in the attack provided the motif for the next tattoo to decorate one of Bryn's limbs. Having tattooed so much of his body, the young man was forced to retreat to the extremity of his limbs in order to find space for a new chapter in his life and he had reached the ankle on his right leg. There was more empty space on his left leg but this was bruised and bloodied from a kicking by the mysterious hooded figures in the late night attack.

Enquiries were held by the police but no one was found to have been wearing hoods in the local pub that night. It seems rather harsh that a young man should receive a duffing up merely for telling stories. After all, our fair isle is prized for its storytellers and bards and for its love of stories. It seems a little out of proportion to inflict beatings on the tellers of stories merely on the grounds that they tell offensive stories, but this it seems is to be the fate of unlucky storytellers. Thus storytellers beware, do not tell stories that will make you unpopular.

There is still an old set of stocks in the yard of Bryn's local pub. If the boy must be punished for his tall stories, it would seem much more humane simply to have him put in the stocks and throw rotten tomatoes and bad eggs at him. But I suppose the local youths, fearing they would be refused permission from village elders to inflict a medieval kind of punishment on him, chose instead to duff up their victim in the dark.

After this unseasonable beating, Bryn put in an appearance one more time at the local, in the lunch hour, but as he made his way to the cigarette machine he noticed shoulders and backs appearing in front of him, and when he stumbled over a foot carelessly lying in the gangway the room fell silent. Unwelcome in the pub, the poor lad took to buying bottles from the off-licence and supermarket and drinking at home instead.

CHAPTER 21

DOLPHIN RESCUES

List of contents:-
Dai's memory leaks.
The five foot long baby.
Why the Catholic priest wears a hat and veil.
Death by vacuum cleaner and how the priest prevents it.
Why bees waggle their bottoms.
The dangers of mocking men of the cloth.

*

Since his stroke Dai's memory has sprung leaks like the old tin bath in the field that the cows drink from. He attempts to reconstruct his memory, painfully, by observation, asking questions, reading books, making lists. At the bottom of the stairs he recalls something he needs from upstairs. On reaching his bedroom he cannot remember why he has climbed the stairs.

Gwyneth takes her father round by the arm, naming the animals. Her father writes them on his lists. When Anni clears away the breakfast dishes she finds lists of words, ideas and names under the table cloth. "Salt shaker, Erin (the cow), Min (Anni's new dog), milk quotas, milk subsidies, broken tractor clutch, shoot the fox, dolphins in the bay."

Only the fox is up for shooting. The dolphins are not to be shot except on film. The Llewellyn-Jones family spotted a pod of dolphins out in Holyhead bay, as many as twelve leaping from the waters, heading towards the Skerries lighthouse. The numbers of dolphins and seals to be viewed off the shores of Ynys Môn in the grey-blue sea of the Angles is growing with the increase in climate temperature.

The Moelfre lifeboat has lately been occupied in rescuing a baby dolphin stranded on the sands of Red Wharf Bay. This five foot long baby gasping helplessly on the shore was discovered by a local who called for assistance; and the blunt nosed infant was lovingly wrapped in a tarpaulin and taken 2 miles out to sea in the lifeboat which is more used to plucking bodies from the sea than depositing them back in the water.

Having become attached to its rescuers and deciding that it no longer liked the look of the icy grey sea in winter, the huge baby attempted to leap back in the boat. The rescuers were obliged to fend it off for its own good. After levelling the wobbling boat, the heroic life-boaters normally engaged in rescuing mammals of the human variety rather than dolphins, were forced to encourage it to go and look for its real parents.

The sight of a pallid dolphin with cracked grey skin gasping for breath is no advert for Anglesey waters and beaches, and the dolphin rescuers performed a noble deed in returning the large nipper to its watery environment, although the story of the baby dolphin's disconsolate grey form following the boat back towards shore brought a tear to the eyes of locals who heard about the rescue.

Or at least the dolphin rescue brought a tear to the eye of Father Tristan, no longer Father to the community but beekeeper and seller of honey. Since hanging up his priestly vestments and black soutane, he had begun wearing new attire: A hat and veil to be precise. He was not wearing his new wife's clothes, but rather had adopted the garb of a white bee suit, together with yellow wellies and yellow gloves.

On summer evenings in his white cottage with Sister Glenys, he enjoyed the smell of honey perfume wafting from his hives and relished gathering the honey harvest far more than he had enjoyed counting the coins from the collection, or sitting up on Saturday nights with his forehead creased into a frown attempting to think of wise words for his congregation in his Sunday homily.

The priest's first swarm of bees came from the Llewellyn-Jones's hives, and he watched the bees building the comb for storing their honey. When the queen began laying her eggs in the comb, he thought of the fat bee he had rescued from a dusty death in the vacuum cleaner. It is said that Father Tristan produces the sweetest and most aromatic honey on the island, and though it is truly said that the temperament of the beekeeper is a key ingredient in the final taste of the honey, the patch of flowers from which the bees gather their pollen is even more crucial in forming the amber syrup.

The incomparable taste of Fr Tristan's honey and the proximity of his hives to Anni's magical herb and flower garden on the Llewellyn-Jones farm is no coincidence. On their first flight, Fr Tristan's scout bees made straight for Anni's garden and the ones who came back fat with delicious nectar began their bee dance, telling the other bees where to find the source of a heavenly meal.

The clumsy figures of eight and bottom swaying of the bee waggle dance were a joy to behold, and as Fr Tristan put on his bee suit with its elasticated cuffs and elasticated legs which fitted close to his welly boots so that he did not find any unexpected bees in his trousers, creeping into delicate parts of his anatomy, he felt himself to be the happiest beekeeper in the world.

To tell the truth, the priest was glad to hang up his long frock-like vestments and his soutane. He had sometimes been taunted by boys in the village for, "Wearing a dress," since most of the village boys were Chapel and not Catholic and had no idea of the dignity of his religious dress and its long traditions.

One would think that the story of the prophet Elijah who blasted a bunch of men, who annoyed him on a hill, with divine fire, and burnt them to a crisp, might serve as a cautionary tale for those tempted to ridicule men of the cloth. Not to mention the prophet Elisha, who inherited Elijah's mantle, and who ordered wild bears to gobble a few village boys who had decided to while away a boring hour by shouting insults at the priest and telling him to, "Go up slap head."

One would imagine that those tempted to scoff at ministers of God would exercise more caution, if only to avoid meeting a similar fate. The tormentors of Elisha were torn to bits by wild animals; a salutary warning against insulting a man of God you would think. However, Tristan had meekly put up with cross-dresser jokes and taunts about women's clothing for years from the little ruffians who leaned over his gate to shout at him and then ran away from the consequences.

As a little aside here, I have often wondered how prophets got to be prophets. Although they are largely self-appointed, by definition they must have a following, some people who believe in their prophecies or they wouldn't be prophets. It makes you wonder how some of the more unpleasant ones amongst them, those who threaten dire happenings, ever managed to curry popular favour. Elisha isn't the kind of guy I'd want to meet socially. And I'm not big on St Paul to tell the truth – something about his attitude to women.

I don't mind the Jesus fellow so much, he seems much more like an ordinary bloke, the sort who turns up with wine at a party and hangs out with the liberal crowd, the non-judgmental sort who doesn't mind it when the girl pours expensive aftershave or perfume, whatever it was, over him instead of giving the money to Oxfam.

Prophets may be the acknowledged legislators of the world but I'm with the poet Shelley when he said, "Poets are the unacknowledged legislators of the world." Poets are a much gentler breed than prophets. When did you last read in the newspaper of a poet calling fire and brimstone down for someone abusing his poetry?

Religion and prophets and whatnot are the sorts of things I sometimes think about when I'm brushing my teeth and I've got nothing else to do. I suspect this is one of the ill-effects of having a vicar for a near father-in-law. I sometimes mull over these mysteries of life in the queue at the supermarket where I always seem to be unlucky. Even if there is only one person in front, I notice that statistically I'm very unlucky in being stuck nine times out of ten behind the person whose tinned tomatoes or canned pie has lost its barcode, and I have to wait whilst they ring the bell for the assistant who has to fetch another one and takes ages because the customer can't remember which aisle it came from.

I try to avoid the supermarkets when I can, and shop at the farm shop, because of the pernicious effects that a notice beside the checkout till is having on shoppers. The poster draws attention to the fact that if a customer needs an item of shopping that she has forgotten to put in her trolley, once the rest of her goods are on the conveyor belt, she can have an assistant bring it for her.

I have noticed on a number of occasions, shoppers getting tired halfway down their shopping lists, going to the till with their incomplete shopping, and then asking an assistant to bring the rest for them. One Saturday morning I had chance to read most of *The Times* in the queue while I was waiting for a customer in front who had apparently forgotten four items from her list, which gave me time to wonder why she didn't just hand in her shopping list at the door and sit in the car or the supermarket café and wait for the staff to bring all her shopping.

CHAPTER 22

RURAL LIVING

List of contents:-
How many miles do you get after the petrol light comes on?
Fetching a petrol can and a siphon.
The café with no food but with an obliging waitress.
A craving for a salami sandwich with a black pepper rind and
plenty of salad cream.
Why 24 hour shops are a good thing; and the fish finger
sandwich.

*

The problem with rural living is the distance between places
and the frequent use of the car and vast consumption of
petrol. One is not always wise enough to stop at a petrol
station when one is passing, even if the petrol gauge is low,
especially on cold winter evenings returning from work. It is
always tempting in the wind and rain to say, "Tomorrow I
will fill up with petrol." But then, you know how it is, late
for work, and a few cars queuing at the pumps, so you put it
off again. I have been caught short a couple of times in this
way.

Once I asked Martyn, my better half, "How many miles
do you get from when the petrol light comes on until the car
comes to a stop?"

He said, "Fifty" without looking up from the book he
was reading. I took him at his word, but having driven forty
six miles and finding myself only three miles from a petrol
station the car came to a dead stop. He was not best pleased

166

when I called him on his mobile to bring me a can of petrol and a siphon from the garage because I was stranded. Apparently the fifty miles was only a rough rule of thumb and not hard and fast.

The time I ran out of petrol I was on my way to the tea room in Cemaes to meet a friend. The tea room is a small eating place with only 6 tables but nevertheless a pleasant friendly place to eat, with personal service. On arrival we ordered toasted teacakes only to be informed that the waitress had to, "Nip out," and buy them fresh at the bakery across the road. It is very pleasant to be served fresh food so we made no objection at all.

On ordering bacon rolls we were told that the waitress had to, "Nip out," again for baps as there were none in the kitchen. I believe that the order of bacon and milk also occasioned a trip out of the café since there appeared to be none on the premises. I have been to seafood restaurants where one is expected to choose one's own lobster from the tank, but I had never before been to a café where one could order bread and milk and have it brought fresh on the instant.

If the scones, bread and teacakes came fresh and hot from the bakery, perhaps the milk and cream were being got fresh from the cows in the locality I enquired? I hardly dared asked for the jacket potato with prawns lest it should occasion a trip to the harbour for the prawns and an almighty bother of cooking and peeling. Though, as it turned out, the milk was merely fresh from the local convenience store and not from the farm; thus I daresay it would have been okay to ask for prawns since they would probably have been fetched from the deep freeze in the general store in the high street.

I commented that it seemed to be an unusual way of running a café and asked whether every customer who placed an order was privileged to have the waitress go out and shop for fresh food on every occasion. However, it seems that being dead of winter, and not the tourist season, there was no reason for the café to expect any customers and so the food was bought on an ad hoc basis when needed.

I considered asking the waitress, as she was nipping out anyway, whether she couldn't get me something that wasn't on the menu but which I knew could be had in the high street, because I actually fancied a sandwich made of salami with black peppered rind, absolutely smothered in salad cream. You know how there are times in life you'd perform almost any action to get your hands on something? Like the Milk Tray man of the old adverts, who jumped ravines and swam shark infested waters to bring chocolates to his lady love, you feel sometimes that it would be well worth the bother of driving twenty miles for a bar of chocolate.

Nowadays even the Spar near Holyhead is open all night, although it is a bit of a hassle that you can't go in and browse the bars of chocolate after 10 pm because they lock the doors and you have to shout through a small window to tell the man what you want. If, like me, you can't think of every brand of chocolate unless they are there in front of you, it's in the nature of a disappointment to have to shout, "Chocolate drops," or "Chewing nuts," through the window so you don't hold up anyone coming behind you, and then find that really you asked for the wrong thing. And as you start walking towards the car, and even more so when you are driving along the road, you suddenly regret that you didn't say, "Turkish delight," or, "Rum and raisin fudge."

When paying, you put your pennies in a metal box on your side of the window, just like you do in the bank, and the man puts the chocolate bar in the box on his side of the window, and when he has got the pennies you get your chocolate.

Still I am very grateful that we have a few open-all-night places on our isle because I can remember back twenty years ago when a friend of mine stepped off the midnight ferry coming from Ireland and badly wanted a fish fingers on toast

168

sandwich before going to bed. He trudged for miles around Holyhead looking for the, "All night shop," seeing nothing but the stars until 3 am when a policeman on the beat popped out of the shadows and asked him where he was going.

My friend was astonished to find that there was no such thing as a 24 hour shop in the vicinity and he had to do without his fish finger toastie that night. I must say, as a warm and comforting supper, it's hard to beat a fish finger sandwich, unless it's a chip butty, or possibly a sandwich of ready salted crisps. Dear Martyn's preference is for meat pie sandwiches, either beef and gravy pies, or Cornish pasties – provided they are flat pasties and not the humped stegosaurus type which is rather inconveniently shaped to put between two slices of bread, and requires too big a stretch of the mouth for comfort, though it can be done.

CHAPTER 23

LYING DEAD IN THE ROAD

List of contents:-
Aled Hughes annoys his mother by drying his hands on the bathroom towel.
The boy who played chicken and lived.
Aled Hughes eats twelve brown buttons.
Inspecting the motion.
Anwen Hughes gobbles buttercups.
A six year old tries a spot of decorating.

*

Aled Hughes, Dr Hughes's son, has soured in temper since being deprived of his shooting practice with Eirian the lawyer's husband. He has taken to annoying his mother by deliberately drying his hands on the bathroom towels.

"Don't dry your hands on the towels in the bathroom, dear," she admonishes him. "Use the towels in the kitchen."

"It's a long walk from the bathroom to the kitchen," the lad grumbles. "Why should I?"

"Keep the towels nice for guests, dear," she instructs.

In fact there are very few guests privileged enough to use the beautiful towelling rectangles laid out with artistic precision in the bathroom. Members of the extended family, neighbours, familiar guests are politely requested not to disturb the arrangement of expensive towels after they have used the loo and washed their hands but to, "Step into the kitchen," and dry their hands on towels hung over the kitchen radiator. The bathroom towels are only for guests higher up the social scale than the Hughes family.

In defence of Aled, it was indeed more than a step to the kitchen from the bathroom because the Hughes's bungalow was vast. On giving her address to people she didn't know, Mrs Hughes always said that she lived in, "Rhydwyn. The better part," by which she meant one of the larger bungalows overlooking the bay and not the council estate.

Aled had always been a difficult boy. Why two such troublesome children as Aled and Anwen should be given to irreproachable parents like the doctor and his wife is hard to fathom. The apposite phrase by the author of *King Lear*, "How sharper than a serpent's tooth it is to have a thankless child," springs to mind at this juncture.

As a child one of Aled's favourite games was playing chicken, running across the road in front of cars, daring them to stop in time. When he could not get anyone to play with him, he happily played this game by himself for hours at a time. There were very few children in fact who would play this game with him for any length of time due to Aled's belief in his own immortality. He was absolutely convinced that, thanks to the favour of the gods and the Tylwyth Teg, he could escape the wheels of any vehicle no matter how close it was when he began his dash across the road in front of the approaching bonnet.

Despite having been hit and somersaulted over the bonnet of one car in his youth, he still did not give up the game. He attributed the fact that he was more or less unscathed on that occasion, apart from a few bruises, to his own favoured status as the beloved of the gods. Although he had turned a perfect revolution in the air over the bonnet and landed in the hedge on the other side of the road, he was not deterred from playing chicken.

It was only a few months after the incident of the somersault that a boy of eleven ran into Mrs Hughes's kitchen to say, "Please, Mrs Hughes, Aled is lying dead in the road."

Again, however, thanks to divine favour, the wretched boy was not dead but merely knocked out by a glancing blow from the wing of a car. He did not even need a visit to hospital since all his bones were still intact and his father the doctor was able to patch up his cuts and grazes.

It is a miracle that a boy who had so many mishaps while playing chicken should live to the age of 21, but that is the age Aled Hughes had reached by Christmas of the year that his sister Anwen had moved out to live with the Cardiff-Jones's.

The Christmas began auspiciously enough for him. Aled swallowed the silver coin he found in the Christmas pudding. It has always been considered lucky to find the shilling in the Christmas pudding and the fortunate boy, who had emerged from a misspent youth of playing chicken, did not merely find the lucky coin but swallowed it into the bargain. If that is not a lucky omen, I cannot think what is.

"It'll pass out the other end," Dr Hughes commented dismissively on Mrs Hughes's anxious query regarding her son having swallowed a silver coin.

"Watch for it in the loo. Don't waste it," was the doctor's comment to his son.

Mrs Hughes was comforted by Dr Hughes pointing out that one silver coin was rather less of an ordeal than the twelve brown buttons he had once passed in a single motion.

To explain the last, I should go back some years to when Aled was five years old and he had swallowed twelve brown buttons from his grandmother's sewing box. Why he should swallow twelve brown buttons with two holes for the thread will perhaps never be known. Perhaps he thought they were sweets, although one would imagine that after swallowing one or two his mistake would have become evident. Whether he just liked the taste of buttons or only wanted to annoy his grandmother is lost in the annals of history, but suffice to say that his poor grandmother was frantic when she discovered that the buttons were missing and where they had gone.

I must confess to feeling a sneaking admiration for the intrepid boy because I cannot imagine that the taste of buttons is very nice, and to eat twelve in a row without even a hint of sickness or indigestion is quite a feat.

His grandmother was instructed to watch any motions passed and to search for the swallowed buttons. They came out whole of course, though rather difficult to spot because they were brown. It required the good lady to do a bit of chopping with a knife and fork in order to find them all. And she conscientiously cut up the said motion and counted twelve before satisfying herself that the lad was in no danger from button poisoning or other internal damage which might be suffered from ingesting brown buttons. Whatever complaints Dr and Mrs Hughes had as parents, it certainly could not be said that Aled Hughes was a fussy eater.

The capacities of a child's digestive system are a constant source of wonder to me. Buttons were not the only strange delicacy that Aled enjoyed as a child. He once swallowed a jar full of newly hatched tadpoles, along with the stagnant pond water, for no particular reason that anyone could discover. And, on a similar theme, he had persuaded his sister Anwen, when she was very small, to eat buttercups on the grounds that, "Cows do it, and it's good for them."

Impressed by her brother's logic, the little girl had followed his example and swallowed as many as twenty buttercups before being discovered by their grandmother and prevented from eating any more. The buttercups stayed down for a while, but Anwen never developed a strong stomach like her brother's, and around 6 o' clock in the evening she turned a funny shade of green and heaved and heaved all over the kitchen floor. After the green complexion came a pallid white one. Fortunately, being of the medical profession, Dr Hughes was always at hand with some noxious though effective medicine. However the poor grandmother was blamed once again for her lack of vigilance.

The unpleasant consequences of a number of the obstreperous boy's pranks were inflicted on Aled's poor grandmother as he was growing up. Frequently called on to babysit or to provide some respite for the parents who had the arduous task of parenting the ungrateful boy, the gentle old lady was ever at hand to be put upon.

At only 6 years of age, having recovered from the affair of the brown buttons, the adventurous lad had tried his hand next at a spot of decorating. When his grandmother was babysitting and had put him safely to bed at 7 o' clock, as she thought, the bad lad had a go at stripping his bedroom of wallpaper.

He started at ground level and by 8 o' clock in the evening he had stripped the paper up to the height of his bed. He got quicker with practice and by 8.30 pm he was up to the level of the window sill. Once he had got the hang of pulling the paper off in long strips, instead of merely pulling off small pieces at a time, he managed it with great dexterity.

By nine in the evening he was nearly to the ceiling and only the corners, which had been firmly stuck down with glue, evaded the stripping. Down the side of his bed the wallpaper lay, with small pieces at the bottom, and huge long strips on top. If the doctor and his wife had been able to view it as the beginning of a career as a painter and decorator, it might have been better for Aled, but instead his parents repapered with the same old flowery paper which had been on before, rather than redecorating with the football wallpaper that Aled vociferously protested he wanted.

His grandmother was in deep disgrace for this episode because his parents blamed her for the loud volume on the television set, "Which must have disguised the tearing noises," as the décor was pulled from the wall.

I must confess to feeling some sympathy for the wall-stripping episode because my niece Eiry has similar tendencies and once, when I was babysitting, I had a nasty surprise on going upstairs to the loo. At the top of the stairs on the landing wall, just about child's eye-level, a big felt-tip graffito of a rather wobbly house with bent walls caught my attention. It hadn't been there when I'd put Eiry to bed. I called her out of bed and said sternly, "Did you do that?"

She came clutching her teddy bear and said, "No," quite crossly.

Well I knew it wasn't her mother who'd done it. In fact I knew my sister was going to be furious about the new wallpaper, and the fact that it was felt-tip made it all worse. But goodness me, even the telling off she got for that drawing didn't stop my niece from doing it again. That girl just couldn't seem to stop herself from scribbling on walls.

In the end, to stop her scribbling over the whole house, my sister told her she could choose just one wall in her own bedroom – which was named the graffiti wall – and she was allowed to scribble what she liked on that wall but on no other. A desperate remedy perhaps but it worked and is perhaps to be recommended to all parents of incurable graffiti artists.

CHAPTER 24

AN ANGLESEY CHRISTMAS

List of contents:-

*

The season began with Morgan and Morwena Davies tying a white Christmas to the back of the old yellow tractor, and it continued with a family flavour.

Old Arwel Davies, eighty in years, and grandfather to Bryn and Morwena disapproved of Morwena moving out of the family home to Bangor.

"Moving out of the house before you get married. Home not good enough for you?" he chuntered from the depths of his armchair in the firelight, when she came back for Christmas.

"You'll get into trouble you will, my girl. Why don't you get married then?"

The old man shook his head until his flat cap seemed in danger of falling from his head. His fingers danced the fandango on the chair arms in his fingerless gloves. Then he got up and shuffled into the kitchen. The black bottomed kettle whistled on the old fashioned range.

There was only one teaspoon visible. It was standing in an opened jar of honey on the table. Arwel was fond of a spot of honey and regularly helped himself to the sweet liquid of the bees which fed on Anni Llewellyn-Jones's magic kitchen garden. He helped himself to a mouthful now, sucking greedily at the spoon while he was making the tea. A small dribble of amber honey dripped from his lips onto his chin.

The old man untucked his shirt from his trousers and wiped the sticky teaspoon on the underside of the cloth. He then spooned the tea into the teapot, poured in the water from the kettle and gave the tea a swirl with the spoon.

Perhaps anxious about using the tea towels too frequently and occasioning himself more washing, whenever Arwel Davies needed cutlery he would carefully wipe wet or dirty spoons or forks on the underside of his shirt which he'd untucked from his trousers for that very purpose.

The cleanliness of the shirt could not always be vouched for unfortunately, which is perhaps why the old man was careful to wipe the cutlery using the underside of his garment rather than the front. Of course it may just have been that he did not wish food stains to appear on his front but, whatever the reason, he could rarely be nagged or persuaded into using a tea towel for the task.

"Cup of tea for you," he announced to Morwena as he came back. He settled into the rocking chair when he returned because the ten ghostly fingers still doing the fandango on the arm rests were annoying him.

Morwena sipped daintily from the edge of the cup.

"Thanks, Gramp," she said. "It's a lovely cup of tea."

The old man rocked. He began to chuckle under his breath. It grew to a cackle.

"Heh, heh . . . heh . . . heh!"

"What is it Grampy?" Morwena asked.

"Heh, heh," the old man cackled. "I put shit in it."

If Morwena did not get the husband she wanted for Christmas, at least Bryn Davies got a dog. He found it wandering in the lanes, shivering from cold and, as it seemed to be an outcast like himself, he felt sorry for the creature and took it to his annexe. He painstakingly wrote a notice, his writing and spelling not being too good, and affixed it to the farmyard gate. It read:

Thorough-bread found in the lane
No collar or tag
But answers to the name Bones

No one came to claim the dog and thus a permanent companionship formed between Bryn and Bones. How Bryn, who was not the brightest of young men, cleverly discovered that the dog's name was Bones I could not have imagined if I had not been told; but it seems that the tattooed boy had tried an endless succession of names, such as Fido, Rover, Lassie, Gelert and Muttley, but got no response from the abandoned creature until he said, "Bones."

It is difficult to write this history in a way that is not disjointed and I apologise to my readers and explain that it is the animated paper clip at the edge of the page in Microsoft Word that keeps winking and blinking at me and raising his eyebrows, which proves quite a distraction at times so that I often lose my place. Sometimes he tumbles into a heap, possibly exhausted by all the winking and blinking he has to do; and at other times he turns into a pair of glasses and looks at me through them.

A friend of mine suggested turning the paper clip off but the sight of his reproachful face when I consider doing such a thing, and watching his eyes start out of his head as though he admires my writing, compels me to feel pity for him. He is observing me now with a quizzical look as though waiting for me to decide whether to keep him in employment or not, but I am so used to his clanking when he falls to bits into a little heap at the corner of my page, as though he is exhausted, I don't think I could bear to be parted from my paper clip at this juncture.

The main annoyance is that having thought a profound thought, one finds it gone, vanished into thin air, never to return, because one has jumped at the clanking sounds the little paper clip man makes when he falls down. But I am gradually learning to pay less attention to his antics, although I do find it distracting when he does something new, like turning himself into three intersecting rings and rolling one eyeball around the rings. It makes me feel rather seasick as the eye approaches me like a rollercoaster heading straight for me, and then rolls away again.

I like it when a light bulb goes on above his head.

"What a bright idea," he seems to be saying, though whether he means my ideas or his own I am never quite sure. In short I would be distressed to lose the companion of my writing hours, even if he does amount only to a paper clip.

Has the mean Jesuit priest learned from last year? It seems some kind of conversion has taken place for when Uncle Jac arrives for Christmas at the Llewellyn-Jones household he has actually brought presents and has even wrapped them in an old newspaper.

"Why thank you for the present, Uncle Jac," Tudur is able to say, accurately this time, as his uncle hands him a bottle that bears some resemblance to a squat bottle of whisky. Tudur is in hope that it may prove to be a mini bottle of Penderyn single malt from the Brecon Beacons or, more likely from the shape of the glass container, a bottle of Brecon Vodka. In fact it is one of the leading brands of spot and blackhead removal liquids.

For Dai there are three lottery scratch cards. The now forgetful Dai looks rather helplessly at the cards.

"Here Dad," Huw produces a coin and helps him to scratch. Scratching the cards leaves a grey crumbly residue on the pristine white tablecloth. None of the numbers are winners.

"Strange," says Uncle Jac. "I nearly always win a pound at least, or a tenner."

179

For Huw there are jump leads because Uncle Jac has a spare set.

Anni's present is a Boots £5 money off voucher but you have to buy some goods to get the money off.

For the younger Llewellyn-Jones's there is a variety of toys collected free from cereal packets.

CHAPTER 25

LOOSE ENDS

List of contents:-
Tying up the loose ends of this history since everyone wants
to know what happens to people in the end.
It is down to Tudur to manage spring this year and get it
fixed to the tractor.
There is another dog to fatten.
The future of the blue-nosed family.
It could be kissing cousins again.
The doctor's gleaming bottom and how he forgets his wife.
The changeling – a baby taken by the fairies.
I dreamt I dwelt in marble halls.

*

It is down to Tudur to manage the spring season this year.
His father is sitting cheerfully by the fire with a blanket over
his knees. From the small table in front of him, Dai picks a
piece of bacon off his plate. He smiles at the tiny Yorkshire
terrier gazing at him from the hearth rug."

"Here then . . . Min? Isn't it Min?" he asks. "Here dog,
catch." He lets a piece of bacon with fatty rind drop towards
the floor. The Yorkie snaps its teeth in the air and catches it,
then licks its nose and settles down with a big sigh by the
fire.

"You're not feeding that dog, are you?" Anni says. "It's
fat enough already."

Tudur starts the tractor. "Come on then, what are you
waiting for?" he says over his shoulder. Huw gives the
season a prod in the rear but there is no need. spring sets off

with alacrity after the tractor and the clippety clop of its feet reaches a gallop after they emerge from the farm track onto the main road. Tudur pulls the willing season along the A5025 with his tractor light flashing. Just before he reaches the turn-off for his last field there is a staccato noise from a horn and a waving arm.

"How on earth did you manage it?" Tudur shouts to the driver of the sports car who is none other than Theo Williams who has passed his driving test at last. A reformed Theo who is now area manager for his drinks company.

The Davies family keep plodding on with their blue noses. It crosses Morgan Davies's mind to wonder about the future of his farm. There has been a Davies farming this land for generations. But there is now no future generation of Davies's. It is down to the picture book boy and Morwena of the pasty ankles to find heirs. But, for the blue-nosed children, marriage and children look like phantasms, like the ethereal spirit which haunts the Davies's home.

The coroner records a verdict of accidental death on Aunt Salie. It is official that she slipped on the stairs and broke her neck. There are no children on Wyn's farm either but there is his nephew Huw Llewellyn-Jones, a born farmer, who cannot inherit his father's farm because Tudur is the eldest. It looks as though the two brothers will be farming adjoining farms and there will be cousins once more living next door to each other.

It seems that Uncle Wyn, along with Uncle Jac, will be joining the Llewellyn-Jones's at the Christmas table since there is no longer an Aunt Salie to cook the festive meal for him.

Tragedy is looming in the Hughes's bungalow where the best doctor on the island is becoming forgetful. The curse of Alzheimer's disease has been growing, like a plant putting out feelers in his mind. Inch by inch his memory becomes ivied over with foliage, obscuring its functions. His mind, like house bricks choked with ivy leaves, disappears in the undergrowth.

His family ignore the symptoms, explain away the lapses until it is no longer possible to do so: Until one night he switches off the light, and with a spectacular moon gleaming on his bottom straddles his wife. At 12.47 am there is a hiatus when the white bottom stops moving. The lamp goes back on and the forgetful doctor looks puzzled for a moment.

"Who are you?" he asks Mrs Hughes.

His memory gives out as though it has been in use far too often and now desires rest. It is not long after this that the doctor's heart gives out too. It had been beating irregularly for some time, as though tired by the strains put upon it.

Father Tristan and Glenys are blessed with a new arrival, the first and last child. A tiny infant, she nevertheless took hours to emerge from her mother. Whether that was because she was a late baby, two weeks overdue, or born to a late mother, or whether she had taken a peep out through the birth canal and taken fright at the lights and sounds, who knows?

Tristan's daughter is christened Gwenllian, and is seized upon by the Tylwyth Teg as she lies in her cradle shortly after birth, and another baby substituted for her. That last part of the sentence is unpleasant and untrue, but Father Tristan dreamed it so it must go in anyway. There is no cure for those born with a pessimistic view of life, they just have to struggle on through it as best they can. And Sister Glenys is always there to hold the bag for him to blow into, and to pat his arm, and to tell him that things are not as bad as they appear.

Aled Hughes is not reformed at all and never will be. He quarrels with his mother over the funeral arrangements for his father. His mother chooses *I dreamt I dwelt in marble halls* for the funeral service. He insists on playing *Angels* by

Robbie Williams instead. Trouble with a capital T came to the funeral in the form of the whole of the Cardiff-Jones clan who have decided to let bygones be bygones now it is too late to do anything about it.

Anwen sits with her brother, tapping her feet . . . . *she offers me protection . . . . a lot of love and affection . . . . I'm seeing angels instead . . . .*

The rendition of *Marble Halls* might have been better suited to the occasion, to the dignity of the deceased who never listened to pop music, and to the grandeur of the Hughes's home, but Robbie Williams wins the day.

The vicar shudders. He will be glad when this horrible day is over.

CHAPTER 26

THE GOD OF FIRE

List of contents:-
Morgan Davies has to wrestle with summer and give it a blow to the head.
There are angels on Holyhead mountain.
Spectacular sunsets in Willesden apparently but not as good as Holyhead.
Another rite of passage.

*

Summer brings misfortune for some this year. Some say it is because Morgan Davies had to wrestle with the season and give it a blow to the head before it would agree to a ride behind his tractor. Morgan's nose gets bluer every year. While the rest of his face turns red from having the sun on his face all day, his nose stays blue.

For others there is better fortune. Although he had grown forgetful like his neighbour Dr Hughes, Dai Llewellyn-Jones remains cheerful, looked after by his wife and family, and Tudur who manages the farm as well as his antecedents from whom the farming gene has been inherited.

Owain Llewellyn-Jones, Tudur's son, now has four teeth and the fifth is about to make its debut in his mouth. He is a remarkable size and weight for his age; and it seems that he is likely to become a man of stature like the Anglesey men of old.

In early summer Owain is joined by a sister, Heledd, who tumbles out of her mother feet first, a breech baby, but none the worse for that. She too shows remarkable early promise, landing on her feet at birth.

Then came midsummer's eve. There was a tinge of yellow in the sky at 5 pm. The yellow spread like an ink stain across Holyhead mountain. And finally the whole mountain was yellow like a glory.

"Look," said Gwyneth to her small nephew. "It's like there's an angel on Holyhead mountain."

"Angel," said the small boy. "Angel on mountain."

They gazed reverentially at the celestial vision.

I watched what looked like the beginning of a spectacular sunset on the mountain. There is a writer, Zadie Smith by name, who has extolled the beauty of Willesden sunsets. I have never seen a Willesden sunset but I am convinced that it has nothing which could rival the beauty of the Holyhead sun dropping behind the mountain, looking for all the world as though a child has dropped and spilt the yellow, orange, pink and red paints from one end of its paint box into the sea.

However this was not a sunset because after yellow, the mountain went red like a blacksmith's furnace and from right across the bay, for miles around, people could see fire torch the sky. Vulcan, the god of fire, was at work on Holyhead mountain.

The younger Llewellyn-Jones's ran down to the end of the garden and stared across the water at the rocky pinnacle.

"Where's Alun?" shouted Rhodri and Gwyneth. "Alun, come and look. The mountain's on fire."

But Tudur and Huw know better than to look for Alun. They passed from boyhood to manhood in the summer ritual.

"My god!" said Huw. "He's gone to the mountain. He's growing up."

"When did Alun go?" bellowed Tudur.

There was an empty place at the dinner table that evening. Alun's seat between Huw and Rhodri remained empty. His bed remained unslept in.

The flames burned for hours into the night. The night was scarlet and black until first light dared peep over the horizon, once the intensity of heat had subsided. And Alun Llewellyn-Jones came back from the mountain a man.

ABOUT THE AUTHOR

C. J. Jones got inspiration for writing this book from living in a house perched on a rocky outcrop on the Isle of Anglesey where an obstreperous pheasant occupied the garden hedge and hedgehogs and badgers used the garden as a thoroughfare. The author once flipped a car onto its roof on the isle during a snowstorm and recalls a bang on the head which may have affected recollection somewhat.